Before she knew wh... someone pushing her to... tumbled to the floor, lan... she cried as she rolled over quickly. "What's the big—" She broke off and gasped.

Something glistened in the clown's outstretched hand. Something shiny.

Something—metallic.

The clown took a step forward, the shoe marked R *coming dangerously near Elizabeth's head.*

"No!" The clerk's voice squeaked with terror. Elizabeth felt her stomach clench. The clown was leaning forward now, his hand stretched ominously toward the clerk. And in that hand—

Elizabeth braced herself and tried desperately not to scream. In the clown's hand was a gun!

SWEET VALLEY TWINS

Elizabeth the Spy

◇

Written by
Jamie Suzanne

Created by
FRANCINE PASCAL

BANTAM BOOKS
NEW YORK · TORONTO · LONDON · SYDNEY · AUCKLAND

To Matthew Markowitz

ELIZABETH THE SPY
A BANTAM BOOK : 0 553 50337 5

Originally published in USA by Bantam Books

First publication in Great Britain

PRINTING HISTORY
Bantam edition published 1997

Conceived by Francine Pascal

Produced by Daniel Weiss Associates, Inc,
33 West 17th Street, New York, NY 10011

Bantam Books are published by Transworld Publishers Ltd,
61–63 Uxbridge Road, London W5 5SA,
in Australia by Transworld Publishers (Australia) Pty Ltd,
15–25 Helles Avenue, Moorebank, NSW 2170,
and in New Zealand by Transworld Publishers (NZ) Ltd,
3 William Pickering Drive, Albany, Auckland.

Printed and bound in Great Britain by
Cox & Wyman Ltd, Reading, Berkshire.

One

"There is absolutely nothing better than Casey's ice cream on a hot day," Maria Slater murmured dreamily, spooning into her hot-fudge sundae.

"Really," Elizabeth Wakefield agreed, taking a long sip from the creamy milk shake in front of her. She and Maria were sitting with several other girls at Casey's ice cream parlor after school. Elizabeth felt the cool, thick liquid slide down her throat. She'd had a tough math test at school that day, and she was happy to indulge herself a little.

"Is there anybody who doesn't want their cherry?" Lila Fowler demanded. "Mine's a little mushed on one side." She fished it out of her sundae with a long-handled spoon and glared at it disapprovingly.

"Not me!" Elizabeth's twin sister, Jessica, took a big lick from her double-scoop chocolate-chocolate chip ice cream and pineapple sherbet cone.

"What's wrong with it, Lila?" Mandy Miller leaned forward curiously. "It looks all right to me."

Lila scowled. "Well, it's kind of hard to see." Gently she turned the cherry around. "There. You have to have really good eyes, of course," she added as Mandy bent closer. "See it now?"

"Well—" Mandy bit her lip.

Maria grinned and nudged Elizabeth. "Typical Lila!" she whispered.

Elizabeth licked her straw and nodded, eyes twinkling. She and Maria didn't usually hang out with Lila and Mandy, who were really Jessica's friends. Elizabeth liked Mandy a lot, but most of the time she thought Lila was pretty silly and snobbish.

On the other hand, Elizabeth told herself, *Jessica thinks my friends are kind of boring and immature. So I guess we're even!*

"Here, Lila. I'll give you a new one. On the house." Joe Carrey, a handsome college student who worked part-time at Casey's, approached their end of the counter. Grinning, Joe fished two cherries out of the cooler and dropped them carefully on Lila's sundae. "There. How's that?" He caught Elizabeth's eye and winked.

Lila's eyes sparkled as she downed all three cherries in one gulp. "Thanks!"

"And typical Joe, wouldn't you say?" Elizabeth nudged Maria back. Joe was Elizabeth's favorite waiter and one of her favorite people these days. Besides working at Casey's and going to school, Joe mowed lawns for extra money and volunteered as a clown at schools and hospitals. He had a great sense of humor, and Elizabeth knew he loved to give away little extras with all the ice cream he served.

In fact, Elizabeth thought as she licked her straw, *Joe's probably the reason why we're all sitting together today.* Both her friends and Jessica's liked hanging out at the counter so they could talk to Joe.

Joe put down his ice cream scoop and wiped his hands on his apron. "Hey, I've got another brainteaser for you girls."

"Another brainteaser? Cool!" Elizabeth's friend Amy Sutton said, waving her cone in the air.

"Brainteasers?" Lila frowned. "What in the world are those?"

"They're a kind of puzzle," Jessica explained. "You tell a story, only you leave out some information. Then the other people have to guess what the whole story is."

"You can ask questions," Elizabeth added. "But the questions have to be answered yes or no."

"Sounds kind of boring," Lila muttered.

"Actually, they're fun," Jessica said. "We've been telling them all week long."

"Well, too bad I missed all the fun," Lila said breezily, tossing her long brown hair over her shoulders. "The things you miss when you take a little vacation in Switzerland."

Elizabeth exchanged amused glances with Amy. Lila was the richest kid in Sweet Valley, and she never missed an opportunity to remind everyone of the pampered life she led.

"Anyway, you guys," Joe spoke up, giving the counter a wipe, "it seems that there were two children born on the same day. They looked absolutely alike, right down to their toenails. They even had the same mother." He paused dramatically. "But they weren't twins. How can that be?"

"Personally, I think the brainteaser *should* be about twins," Jessica said, biting into her cone. "I mean, what could be more interesting?"

Elizabeth grinned at her sister. Most of the time, being a twin *was* a lot of fun. She and Jessica looked so much alike, it was almost impossible to tell them apart—and sometimes they tricked people about which twin was which on purpose. Both sisters had long blond hair, blue-green eyes, and a dimple in one cheek. Elizabeth figured that they probably had the same toenails, too.

Inside, however, the sisters were as different as could be. Each girl had her own hobbies and interests. Jessica loved to talk about fashion, soap operas, and boys with her friends in the Unicorn Club, a group of girls who considered themselves the prettiest and most popular in Sweet Valley Middle School. Elizabeth, on the other hand, spent most of her free time reading a good mystery, having long talks with her close friends, or working on

The Sweet Valley Sixers, the sixth-grade newspaper she edited along with Amy Sutton. But despite their differences, the twins were the best of friends.

"Oh, I know!" Jessica snapped her fingers. "They were born twins, but one of them was adopted when it was little and—"

"Nice try," Joe broke in. "But no. Neither of them was adopted."

"Were they born the same year?" Maria stirred her sundae.

Joe nodded. "Same day, same year," he said with a smile.

"Hmm." Elizabeth tried to think. *Not twins, but—*

"I've got it!" Mandy gasped. "Did one of them— you know, did one of them have an operation to look like the other?"

Joe raised his eyebrows. "Good guess! But no."

Lila cleared her throat. "Was one of them an alien?" she asked importantly.

"You've been reading too many tabloid newspapers!" Joe clapped Lila on the shoulder. "Think hard. You'll get it."

Elizabeth frowned and cast her eyes around the room. The only person who looked exactly like her was Jessica. And, of course, they *were* twins already. *Suppose that Amy looked exactly like me, too,* Elizabeth thought slowly. *Could that happen? And if it could—*

Wait a minute.

Elizabeth pressed her hands to her forehead. She

was onto something, she was sure. "If Amy looked just like me," she said aloud. "Then—"

Jessica wriggled on her stool in mock horror. "Then there'd be three of us!" she said. "Can you imagine? You'd borrow my clothes, and I'd borrow Amy's clothes, and Amy would—"

"Triplets!" Elizabeth burst out, a grin spreading over her face. "It has to be! If Amy looked like me, we'd be a set of triplets. The kids weren't twins— because there was another baby who looked just like them. They were two in a set of triplets!"

"Good for you!" Joe gave Elizabeth a thumbs-up sign.

"Of course." Amy shook her head. "It seems so obvious now."

"It always sounds easy once it's been explained," Joe said as Elizabeth gave her milk shake a stir. "The trick is to figure it out. Congratulations, Elizabeth!"

Elizabeth shrugged. "Well, Jessica kind of gave me the idea," she admitted.

"It doesn't matter," Joe said, grinning. "Just goes to show you, girls, things aren't always what they seem."

Lila rolled her eyes. "I still think one of them should have been an alien."

Elizabeth gave Amy a sideways glance, but her friend was frowning at her ice cream.

"What's this?" Amy spooned something out from her cone. "It looks like a chocolate kiss!" She eyed it suspiciously. "A chocolate kiss in my cone! How would it get in there?"

She stared hard at Joe, who looked up at the ceiling.

"You did it," Amy guessed, pointing a finger at Joe.

Joe thumped his hand against his chest. "Who, me?" he asked innocently.

Amy began to giggle. "Admit it, Joe! You hid it inside my cone on purpose!"

With a smile, Elizabeth watched Joe start to laugh, too. "Just goes to show you," he said. "You didn't expect a chocolate kiss in your cone. But things aren't always the way you expect them to be!"

"Do you have any more problems for us, Joe?" Mandy asked a few minutes later.

Jessica hoped he did. She took another lick of her ice cream. The pineapple sherbet on the top was almost gone, but there was plenty of chocolate-chocolate chip left. *Mmm.* Not to mention plenty of sprinkles. In fact—Jessica blinked to make sure she wasn't seeing things—it looked like Joe had added some extra sprinkles on the inside of the cone, too.

Joe scratched his head. "Well, let's see—"

"Hey! Carrey!" a voice rang out from across the room. "Get to work!"

Jessica spun her stool around to see Jeff Casey, the nephew of old Mr. Casey, who owned the store. Scowling, Jeff rattled a tray. "Forget puzzles! We got customers here!"

Jessica looked around the room. *Customers?* she thought. She could see two old men sitting by the window, and a college student studying on the other side of the room. That was it. "Three customers," she muttered to Lila. "And Jeff thinks it's the biggest thing in the world!"

Joe looked rattled. "Umm—I was just—"

"Yeah, right." Jeff banged down the tray so hard Jessica jumped. "It's a hot enough day out there without adding even more hot air to it. You never wiped up that table." He motioned to a table that Jessica thought looked perfectly clean. "Let's see you bust a little tail here, Carrey. Like me."

Joe's face hardened into a frown. "Just a minute, please," he said firmly. "I'm waiting on these girls."

"Well, it better be quick." Jeff shoved a few dishes onto the tray. The clatter made the college student look up for a moment. Then she sighed and returned to her book.

Jessica nudged Mandy. "Order something else," she hissed.

"Huh?" Mandy swallowed the last bite of her sundae and stared at Jessica.

"I said, order something else!" Jessica couldn't stand to see Joe pushed around like that.

Mandy frowned. "But I don't *want*—"

"Amy would like another ice cream cone," Elizabeth said quickly. Jessica grinned and winked at her sister.

"I would?" Amy asked, frowning.

Joe smiled down at her. "Sure thing, kiddo. What flavor?"

"Umm—rainbow sherbet again, I guess," Amy said doubtfully.

"Rainbow sherbet!" Jeff snorted. "Give me a break."

"Yeah, rainbow sherbet," Jessica agreed. "You *love* rainbow sherbet, don't you, Amy?" She poked Lila. "Kind of juvenile if you ask me," she whispered.

Lila snickered. "Could be worse," she hissed back.

"How?" Jessica raised her eyebrows.

Lila leaned closer. "Pink bubble gum."

Jessica nodded. *Yup, pink bubble gum ice cream would be even more immature. Especially in a cake cone!*

Joe scooped up a little extra sherbet and packed Amy's cone with a flourish. "Anybody else?" he asked hopefully.

"Umm—how about a cup of water?" Jessica asked, stealing a glance back toward Jeff. She felt a tingle of satisfaction to see his face was turning red.

"Coming right up." Joe reached for a glass.

"So when do you do your clown act next, Joe?" Elizabeth asked curiously.

Joe smiled and filled the glass with ice. "In two days," he told her. "I've got a performance at a day-care center."

"Oh, that should be fun," Amy said enthusiastically.

Jessica was about to nudge Lila, but she changed her mind. Clowns were kind of juvenile, of course, but she'd seen Joe's act once—well, maybe two or three times—and he was pretty good, she had to admit.

Elizabeth pushed her milk shake away and propped her arms on the table. "Tell us your secret, Joe. Where do you find the time to do all these things?"

"Time?" Joe raised his eyebrows. "Well—"

"Carrey!" Jeff spat out the word. "You working here or not?"

A pained expression appeared on Joe's face. "I'll be right back." He handed Jessica her glass. Then, with a quick motion, he slid out from behind the counter.

Jessica turned to watch. An unpleasant smile spread across Jeff Casey's face.

"What a jerk," she murmured to Mandy, making sure Jeff couldn't hear her. "I bet anything *he* doesn't put extra sprinkles on the inside of ice cream cones!"

"OK, guys," Elizabeth announced a few minutes later. The sunlight streaming through the windows of the ice cream parlor had reminded her of another brainteaser she'd heard once. Anyway, she wanted to get her mind off the way Jeff was treating Joe. "Here's a puzzle for you."

"Oh, good," Mandy said.

Lila sniffed. "Is it about aliens?" she wanted to know.

"No." Elizabeth smiled. "But it does take place in an ice cream parlor." She swung her stool around to face the other girls. "A man comes into an ice cream parlor at almost twelve o'clock," she said in her spookiest voice. "He isn't carrying a flashlight, and he doesn't turn on any lights. But . . ." She held up one finger dramatically in the air.

"But what?" Jessica asked with a frown.

Elizabeth swiveled to see if Joe was listening. He was cleaning a table with a damp cloth, wearing his usual outfit—a white T-shirt and black corduroy pants. *How can he stand to wear long pants on a hot day like this?* Elizabeth shuddered.

"Go ahead." Joe dipped the cloth into a bucket of suds. "I can hear you."

Elizabeth cleared her throat, focusing on the story again. "So it's almost twelve o'clock, and he doesn't touch the light switch. And yet somehow he's able to make a double-scoop mint chocolate chip and coffee ice cream cone in less than thirty seconds."

"Yuck." Jessica wrinkled her nose. "That sounds totally disgusting."

"I didn't ask if it was disgusting," Elizabeth said smoothly. "The question is, how did he do it?"

For a moment, no one spoke. Then Amy leaned forward. "If it was almost midnight—," she began doubtfully. "Well, I mean—was he blind?"

Maria snapped her fingers. "Hey, that makes sense! Then he wouldn't need any light at all," she said. "He'd be used to doing things in the dark."

Elizabeth shook her head. "Nope."

"Umm . . ." Jessica scratched her head. "You said

he didn't turn on the lights. Did a friend turn them on for him?"

"That would be pretty sneaky," Elizabeth admitted. "But that's not the answer."

"Sounds like he was a burglar," Lila murmured.

"Were the lights already on?" Mandy ventured.

"No. But you're on the right track." Elizabeth tried to keep a poker face. She wanted her friends to figure it out, but at the same time, it was also lots of fun to keep them guessing.

There was a footstep behind her. "Do the flavors matter?"

"Joe!" Elizabeth had forgotten all about him. Quickly she spun her seat to face him. But she pushed too hard. With a crash she flew off the whirling stool and stomped firmly on Joe's left foot. Elizabeth drew in her breath and steadied herself against the counter. "Oh, Joe, I'm so sorry! Are you all right?"

"Just fine." Joe didn't even move as Elizabeth climbed back onto her stool. "No big deal."

Elizabeth bit her lip. "Are you sure?" she asked.

Joe shrugged. "Really—no problem."

"Well, OK. But I'm sorry, anyway," Elizabeth apologized again, hoping it wasn't possible to die of embarrassment.

Joe emptied the soapsuds down the sink. "So do the flavors matter?"

"Umm—no," Elizabeth answered, forcing herself to think about the puzzle. "They could be any flavors."

"The guy you're talking about was probably Joe." Startled, Elizabeth looked up. Jeff was standing over her, his eyes flashing angrily. "Sure," he went on, as if to himself. "Joe knows his way around here, all right. He could make a cone in the dark, if he wanted. Sure!" He gave a brittle laugh.

"But let me warn you, *buddy*," he continued, turning to Joe and narrowing his eyes, "this store doesn't belong to you. Yet! You come here at midnight for ice cream, you better pay for it. Hear me?" He glared menacingly at Joe.

Elizabeth bit her lip anxiously as Joe stared back at Jeff, hardly moving a muscle. After a moment, Joe calmly folded his arms across his chest. "Uh-huh," he said in a low voice, not taking his bright blue eyes off Jeff's. "I hear you."

There was silence.

Elizabeth sucked in her breath. For a moment she was afraid that Jeff might start a fight. "Umm—," she began, but the words seemed to catch in her throat. "I mean—" She swallowed hard. "This puzzle isn't—isn't about Joe."

Nobody spoke.

"In fact, you're all making an assumption that you probably shouldn't be making," Elizabeth added lightly, her voice picking up confidence as she spoke. "Even you made that mistake," she added, pointing to Jeff with what she hoped was a steady finger. Just in case he might take that the wrong way, she gave a silly little laugh. "Imagine! Jeff Casey—making a mistake!"

Jeff made a noise deep in his throat. Turning his head slowly, he stared at Elizabeth. Elizabeth felt her cheeks go red. She hadn't meant to sound sarcastic.

"Yeah, right," Jeff said after a moment. "Let me tell you, kid, Jeff Casey's not one to make mistakes."

"Umm, yeah, right, of course, but—," Elizabeth began in a very small voice, when Maria suddenly snapped her fingers.

"I've got it!" she crowed. "What time of day is it when it's almost twelve o'clock?"

Amy frowned. "Well, it's nighttime. Almost midnight."

"The end of the day," Mandy put in.

"Obviously." Lila sniffed. "I mean, duh."

"Right." Maria stuck a finger in the air triumphantly. "That's what Elizabeth wanted us to think, with that ghostly voice she put on and all the stuff about not turning lights on. But what's the *other* time of day when the clock's almost at twelve?"

"Oh, man!" Jessica sank down against the counter. "Twelve o'clock noon," she muttered. "Of course!"

"It was morning," Amy breathed. A smile began to cover her face. "The guy came in during the day!"

"So of course he didn't use any lights," Maria finished for her.

"Exactly!" Elizabeth exclaimed.

"No fair!" Lila grimaced and stood up. "You definitely said it was almost twelve o'clock at *night*. I heard you."

Elizabeth shook her head. "I never said that—

you guys just assumed it." She smiled at Lila. "See, that's what makes the puzzle so tricky."

Lila tossed her hair over her shoulder. "Whatever. I still think these puzzles would be more fun if they had aliens. Did you know that Johnny Buck is thinking about adopting an alien baby? I read that in a newspaper when I was in Switzerland," she added proudly.

Elizabeth couldn't hold back her laughter. "That sounds like a really serious newspaper!"

Lila turned a little red. "What are you trying to say, Elizabeth?"

Elizabeth bit her lip. She *did* think Lila sounded pretty silly, but she didn't especially want to start a fight. "All I'm saying is, well—umm . . ."

Joe clapped her lightly on the back. "Nice brain-teaser, Elizabeth!" he told her, coming to her rescue. "I'll have to remember that one. You really had me wondering there!"

Elizabeth smiled back at him. "Thanks, Joe."

Joe's a really neat guy, she thought happily. Then she caught sight of the angry look on Jeff's face.

She shook her head.

I hope Jeff isn't going to give him any trouble!

Two

$\Diamond$

Elizabeth turned the page in her book. *"Chapter Three: Out of Money!"*

It was close to nine o'clock the following evening, and Elizabeth was sprawled among the pillows on her bed. She was reading a new Amanda Howard mystery novel, featuring her all-time favorite detective, Christine Davenport.

The action was already starting to heat up. Christine had met a friendly young man named Jay Carroll. But as the second chapter ended, it was clear that Jay had a problem he needed to talk to Christine about. "Just tell her, Jay," Elizabeth urged him aloud as she headed into the next paragraph. "Christine's very understanding."

She buried her nose in the book.

"'I—I don't know how to say this,' Jay began, nervously twisting his fingers.

"Christine nodded. 'Take your time,' she told him gently.

"Jay took a deep breath. 'You probably think I'm rich,' he said in a strangled voice. 'Well, I'm not. I need money, and I need it badly. There are business ventures—'

"'I understand,' Christine said comfortingly. Her heart went out to this poor young man. 'Isn't there any—'

"Jay cut her off. 'My aunt,' he said, shaking his head. 'My elderly aunt is quite wealthy. Or so they tell me. I haven't seen her for months. We had a misunderstanding a while back.' He bowed his head and stared fixedly at the floor.

"Christine nodded and came to a decision. 'You need to visit your aunt,' she said, rising gracefully from her chair. 'Once you explain the situation, I'm sure she can't refuse.'

"'Oh, I couldn't.' Jay's face looked tortured.

"'Nonsense,' Christine assured him. 'I'll take care of the details. Give me her telephone number, and I—'"

"Elizabeth!" Panting, Jessica dashed into the room, a flustered look on her face. "We have to go down to the pharmacy right away! I mean, like, now!"

Elizabeth sighed and looked down at the unfinished chapter in front of her. "Umm—can't it wait?"

Jessica shook her head emphatically. "No way! We're completely out of sanitary napkins, there aren't any anywhere in the whole house, and, well . . ." Her voice trailed off.

"Can't you send Mom?" Elizabeth asked.

Jessica dived into Elizabeth's closet and pulled

out a baggy pink sweater with Elizabeth's initials in the corner. "Mom's not home. Neither is Dad."

"Jessica, that's the third sweater you've borrowed from me this week." Elizabeth put down her book.

"Well, I can't find anything to wear," Jessica told her.

Elizabeth rolled her eyes. "If you'd just pick the clothes up off your floor once in a while—"

"Elizabeth, I can't believe you're talking about sweaters at a time like this." Jessica pulled Elizabeth's sweater over her head.

Elizabeth frowned. "But I—"

"The point is," Jessica continued, "Mom and Dad are both gone. You want me to send Steven down to the pharmacy instead?"

Elizabeth thought of their older brother going and buying— "I see your point," she admitted, suppressing a giggle. "But couldn't you go by yourself?" she asked, looking longingly at the book in her lap. "I mean—"

"You'll use them, too," Jessica pointed out, putting her hands on her hips. "It's only fair."

Elizabeth clutched her book to her chest. "Just a little while longer," she begged. "Christine Davenport's about to give this friend of hers some advice, and I really want to find out—"

"*Now*," Jessica said, a note of desperation in her voice. She grabbed Elizabeth's hand and started to tug her off the bed. "The pharmacy closes in twenty minutes!"

Elizabeth sighed loudly. "All right, all right. You don't have to pull."

Luckily, she thought, *the store should be pretty empty this time of night.*

At least we can be anonymous!

Jessica led the way into the drugstore. She was glad she'd borrowed Elizabeth's sweater. The temperature had dropped quite a bit over the last few hours. "Last aisle on the right," she muttered, heading in that direction.

Elizabeth tagged along slowly. "Hey, Jess?"

Jessica stiffened. "Don't use my name, please," she said in a low voice.

Elizabeth frowned. "But—"

Jessica whirled around. "I said, shh!" she hissed. Checking to make sure that no one was watching, she grabbed the nearest box of extra-absorbent maxipads and strode purposefully toward the checkout counter, hoping to get there before she lost her nerve.

Then she stopped and thrust the box behind her back.

"What's wrong?" Elizabeth asked, frowning.

"Oh—nothing," Jessica said brightly. "I just thought, you know, maybe I'd take a few minutes and check through the magazine rack." She flashed Elizabeth her prettiest, most innocent smile. "They might have a *Fashion World Semi-Weekly* I've missed, or something. So . . ."

Elizabeth's frown grew deeper.

"Well, I just thought," Jessica said quickly, "maybe you could stand in line and pay for these. I'd give you the money and everything," she added. "While I looked through—you know." She held the box out toward her sister, a pleading expression on her face. *Look sad, Jessica,* she commanded herself. *Look really, really sad!*

Elizabeth burst out laughing. "Nice try, Jessica," she said. "I'll be happy to wait with you. But you pay."

Jessica knew when she was beaten. "All right," she said grumpily as they took their place in line behind a woman in a white jogging suit. Carefully she turned the box so the logo on the front faced her chest.

The clerk handed a bag to the woman in the jogging suit. "Thanks a lot," he told her in a bored voice. "Have a nice day."

The woman nodded and stepped back. Quickly Jessica took a step back herself, giving the woman plenty of room. But as the woman headed out the door, Jessica's heel thunked against something hard. "Ow!" someone cried.

Startled, Jessica turned around—and let out a low gasp.

A clown stood behind her, grabbing his leg in pain and hopping up and down. She took another look, her eyes nearly bugging out. A clown, in full costume, at almost nine o'clock at night! Her gaze traveled from the fright wig over his hair, to the ton of makeup on his face, right down to the blue-and-red outfit and the humongous brown shoes he wore on his feet.

"Watch where you're going, huh?" The clown moaned, still rubbing his shin.

Jessica stepped back. "I'm, I'm really sorry—sir," she stammered. *Were you supposed to call a clown "sir"?*

"How'd you like it if I kicked you?" The clown glared at Jessica.

"My sister didn't mean to do it," Elizabeth defended her.

The clown grimaced under his heavy makeup. Gingerly he stepped onto his left foot. Jessica noticed that his oversize shoes were marked with the letters L and R. Bending down, the clown massaged his shin just above the shoe marked L. "If it's broken, I'll—" He shook his head and winced with pain.

"I'm really sorry," Jessica said slowly. *Sheesh!* she thought to herself. *I couldn't have kicked him that hard!*

"Next!" the clerk called out, stifling a yawn.

Jessica darted forward and laid the box on the counter. "Just these," she said quickly, trying to remain calm while her heart hammered away inside. She wished the clerk had been a woman. Behind her, she could hear the clown muttering something to himself, but she didn't turn around.

"One box of maxipads," the clerk said in what Jessica thought was an unnecessarily loud voice. "Extra absorbent, huh? That going to be all?"

Jessica started to respond, but she felt someone pushing her from behind.

"Out of the way!" the clown cried.

With a shriek, she dropped to her knees.

Before she knew what was happening, Elizabeth felt someone pushing her to the side. Losing her balance, she tumbled to the floor, landing hard on her shoulder. "Hey!" she cried as she rolled over quickly. "What's the big—" She broke off and gasped.

Something glistened in the clown's outstretched hand. Something shiny.

Something—metallic.

The clown took a step forward, the shoe marked R coming dangerously near Elizabeth's head.

"No!" The clerk's voice squeaked with terror. Elizabeth felt her stomach clench. The clown was leaning forward now, his hand stretched ominously toward the clerk. And in that hand—

Elizabeth braced herself and tried desperately not to scream. In the clown's hand was a gun!

"Do as I tell you and no one'll get hurt," the clown said in a menacing voice.

The clerk stifled a scream. Next to her, Jessica let out a soft moan.

"Fill this bag with all the cash you got." The clown spoke quickly. Elizabeth thought she could see the gun twitch in his hand. She sucked in her breath and shut her eyes. Despite herself, Elizabeth found her eyes snapping open again. The clerk seemed to be taking an awfully long time to do what the robber wanted.

"Now!" The clown jabbed the barrel of the gun toward the clerk's face. Elizabeth suppressed a scream.

"That's all?" The gunman asked as the clerk handed him the money.

"That's—that's everything," the clerk replied weakly.

"Your pockets, then," he barked at the clerk.

Elizabeth's heart was thundering in her chest. Jessica was crying now, great heaving sobs as she lay next to Elizabeth in a bundle on the floor.

I've got to stay calm, Elizabeth told herself. She strained to focus on the gunman. *If I get out of this mess, maybe I can help identify him*, she thought. A tear trickled down her cheek. *If I ever get out—*

Not if I get out! Elizabeth clenched her fists. *When I get out. And trying to identify the robber is exactly what Christine Davenport would do!*

She gazed up. It was hard to see from that angle, but she could clearly make out the blue-and-red costume towering over her. There was a big yellow button near the clown's stomach, too, and then there was a fright wig at the top.

"Faster!" the clown commanded. Elizabeth forced herself to keep looking. The clown makeup looked like it had been put on too quickly. From down below, anyway, the mouth seemed to be on a little crooked. Elizabeth shifted her eyes and stared hard at a piece of red fringe on the clown's chest.

She bit her lip. Something was bothering her—but she wasn't quite sure what.

The clown stepped back. "All right, everybody," he hissed. Elizabeth could see the gun probing through the air. With a sinking heart, she realized the gunman was aiming it directly at her sister!

"You shut up. Got it?" the robber demanded.

"Y-yes. Yes, sir." Jessica's voice shuddered.

"Good enough." The robber stepped back. Now Elizabeth could see a blue canvas bag in his hand. "Don't move. Count to one hundred after I'm gone. And one more thing," he added as he clumped over to the pharmacy door. "Nobody remembers me. Nobody knows what I look like. Got it?" Without waiting for an answer, he was out the door.

"One." Elizabeth could hear the clerk's voice catch. "Three. I mean, two. Three. Four . . ."

Elizabeth moved her aching leg a little. "Are you all right, Jess?" she asked gently, not daring to turn around.

The only answer was a muffled sob, and Elizabeth felt a wave of sympathy and helplessness mixed in with her lingering panic.

She knew that whether she wanted to or not, she'd probably be seeing that clown costume in her dreams for the rest of her life. She could still picture those massive brown shoes coming down nearly on top of her head—the bright red L and the green ʀ. Not to mention the fright wig, the blue-and-red clown suit with the oversize yellow button and the fringe, and—

Hmm.

Elizabeth caught her breath. She could feel a sense of dread creeping up her body.

"It can't be," she muttered to herself.

But as much as she wanted to, she couldn't deny it.

She was almost positive she'd seen that clown costume somewhere before.

Three

◇

"He was pretty tall, I guess," Jessica ventured, wrinkling her nose. It was later that same night, and the twins were sitting in the police station, waiting for their parents to come pick them up.

The police officer nodded. "How tall? As tall as me, say? Taller?"

"Umm . . ." Jessica tried to think back. She was surprised by how much she remembered about the robbery. Kicking the clown in the shin . . . and then being pushed to the floor . . . and watching while the robber leveled his gun at the clerk . . . and . . .

Jessica shuddered. *At least I didn't start to cry or anything*, she thought virtuously, stealing a quick glance at her sister. *Unlike some people I could mention!*

At least, she didn't *think* she'd been crying. Not very hard, anyway.

"Any idea?" The officer raised his eyebrows.

Jessica sighed and shook her head. "Just—pretty tall." She cleared her throat. "Of course, it's hard to tell how tall people are when you're lying on the floor."

The officer nodded.

"There's a lot more I *do* remember," Jessica went on quickly, shifting position on the hard folding chair where she sat. "Like, he was wearing a red-and-blue clown suit, and there was this fright wig, and this kind of fringy-looking stuff." She turned to Elizabeth. "Remember?"

Elizabeth swallowed hard. "Well—only sort of," she answered after a pause.

"What do you mean, sort of?" Jessica demanded. "How can you not remember it?"

Elizabeth shrugged. "I just—forgot the details," she said slowly.

Jessica snorted. "You, of all people!" She stared at Elizabeth curiously. *For someone who loves those Christine Daven-whosis mysteries, she sure isn't very observant!*

The policeman stood up. "We're almost ready to let you go, girls," he said gently. "I know it's been a tough time for you."

"You can say that again," Jessica said emphatically.

"Just one more thing," the officer went on. "There was a security camera in the pharmacy, and I'm going to show you the video it took during the robbery." He loaded a tape into a small VCR. "The tape isn't exactly high quality, but maybe it will jog your memory." He pressed the play button. "If you notice anything, yell."

Jessica watched, fascinated, as the screen came to life. "It's like being in the movies!" she said eagerly, nudging her sister. In the foreground of the picture, she could see the woman in the white jogging suit. "We're stars!"

The policeman grinned. "Just watch the tape, OK?"

"That was the woman in line ahead of us," Jessica said. She strained her eyes. "I guess we hadn't gotten there yet."

"Just wait," Elizabeth said tonelessly.

Jessica drew in her breath as two girls appeared in one corner of the screen. "That's us!" she burst out. But the next moment she felt her lips curling with disgust. "That's *us*?" she asked.

When I imagined being in movies, she thought, *I didn't exactly imagine this!*

"What's wrong?" The police officer frowned.

"Oh—nothing." Jessica glared at her image on the screen. There she stood, behind the woman in the jogging suit. Her hair was a total mess, her eyes looked kind of vacant. Elizabeth's baggy sweater with the EW in the corner was all bunched up at the waist. *Where's my strapless ball gown?* she asked herself angrily. *Where's my big song-and-dance number? Where's Jessica Wakefield, the star?*

Elizabeth shook her head and sighed. "That's us, all right," she said. "The clown will be coming from behind, but I don't think you'll be able to see him real well."

Jessica gave her sister a look. "You sound almost happy about that," she commented.

Elizabeth blushed. "No, it's just—I mean—the video quality is kind of poor." She pointed to the screen. "See, our faces are sort of in shadow. You know they're us, but you can't really tell which one is which."

"That's true. Oh!" Jessica watched in dismay as the Jessica on the screen held out the box of maxipads. To Jessica, the box seemed to grow in size till it was about twelve times larger than anything else on the screen. "Oh, man," she whimpered, sliding down deeper into her seat. "I thought I'd hidden those!"

"I beg your pardon?" The policeman leaned closer.

"Never mind." Jessica waved her hand in front of her face. But the box didn't go away. She shifted her gaze to the corner of the screen, forcing herself to focus on the clerk's back. But before she knew it, her eyes were drifting back—back to the box of maxipads in her hand.

The clown appeared behind the girls on the screen. "You can't exactly see much, can you?" Elizabeth said in a bright voice. "And it's only a black-and-white video, anyway. I don't really remember the colors."

"Oh, I do!" Jessica whirled to face her sister, glad

for the interruption. Anything was better than watching the sanitary napkins filling up the whole screen! She turned back to the policeman. "The dark part of the costume there at the top? That was red, and the bottom of the left leg, that was blue. And he had bright blue eyes."

"Very helpful," the officer said, writing furiously. "Anything else?"

"Umm . . ." Out of the corner of her eye, Jessica could see Elizabeth shaking her head frantically. "What in the world do you think you're doing?" she asked her sister loudly.

"Nothing!" Elizabeth bit her lip and sat perfectly still.

Jessica leaned toward her twin. "You were shaking your head at me! Why were you shaking your—"

"I was not!" Elizabeth said, staring hard at the floor.

"Talk later," the policeman interrupted. "Watch the film, please."

"You were, too," Jessica hissed, but she forced herself to focus on the screen. She watched as she kicked the clown right on the shin, above the shoe marked L. *Great. A movie about me being a klutz,* she thought, wrinkling her nose.

Then she watched the clown pull out his gun and push the sisters to the ground. Next, the clerk filled the bag. At last the robber dashed out the door.

Jessica shook her head. Horrible as the whole thing was, it didn't seem quite so frightening on videotape. In fact, Jessica found that she had to concentrate to bring back that feeling of total terror she'd gotten when she was on the floor. "All I feel right now is embarrassed," she muttered, trying hard not to think about the gigantic box of maxi-pads. "Totally, absolutely, one hundred percent—"

"What's that?" The police officer punched the stop button.

"Oh—nothing." Jessica stood up. "So—we can go now?" she asked politely, wondering how she'd be able to sneak back into the police station to burn the tape.

The officer shook his head. "Not just yet," he told her. "Your parents are still on their way. Besides, we'd like you to watch it again."

"You're kidding!" Jessica's hand flew up to her mouth.

"Again!" Elizabeth wailed.

"Again," the policeman repeated. He rewound the tape and pressed play once more. "I know you want to get out of here, but we'd really appreciate it if you could watch it through once more. Maybe two or three times. OK?"

Jessica sagged back in her seat, staring as the woman in the jogging suit made her purchases once again. She knew what was coming next.

Me, she thought miserably, scuffing the floor with her sneaker.

Good old Jessica Wakefield, looking like a total slob, kicking people in the shins like a complete klutz, and worst of all—

She shuddered.

Waving a box of maxipads around like it's a stupid bag of potato chips or something!

" 'Murder? You've been arrested for murder, Jay?' "

Elizabeth reached automatically for another carrot stick and turned the page. It was late afternoon the next day, and she had finally decided to return to her novel. She hoped it would help take her mind off the robbery—and her worries about the clown suit the robber had worn.

Elizabeth lay faceup on the living room couch. The television flickered in the background, but Elizabeth hardly noticed. The show was only a rerun, and she had turned the volume down low.

"Poor Jay!" she muttered, biting into the carrot stick. "Christine will save him. I know she will." She read on.

"Doubt and shock covered Christine's face, but she stood firm. Holding the phone closer to her ear, she spoke again. 'Are the police holding you in custody?'

"The line crackled. 'Yes, Christine,' came the reply. Christine had never heard her new friend sound so depressed. 'My aunt was found this morning. Dead. She'd been—poisoned.'

"Christine drew in her breath. 'How horrible.'

" 'Yes,' Jay agreed. 'And they think I did it. She had been drinking tea—just before she—' His voice broke. 'And she had used the tea leaves to spell out my name. J-A-Y. The police think it's a dying message. That's why I'm here.'

"'A dreadful mistake,' Christine said, reaching for her coat."

Elizabeth reached for another carrot stick. Setting her jaw determinedly, she looked back at the page. "J-a-y spells lots of things, you know," she argued aloud, even though no one was around to hear. "Maybe she saw a blue jay. Or maybe—"

Wrinkling her forehead, Elizabeth tried to think of another meaning of the word "jay." "Or maybe there's another person named Jay," she said. "Whatever. I'm sure Christine will come up with the answer."

On the television, the rerun had ended and the news was about to begin. Elizabeth considered clicking it off, but decided it would be too much trouble. Instead she returned to her reading.

"'And the worst of it is, I inherit my aunt's entire estate,' Jay said glumly. 'The cash, the jewels, the valuable paintings, all of it. The police say that makes me the obvious suspect.'

"'The obvious suspect is not always the true criminal,' Christine said firmly."

"Yay, Christine!" Elizabeth pumped her fist in the air. She loved it when Christine stuck up for the underdog. The beginnings of a brainteaser began to form in Elizabeth's mind. *A woman is poisoned and tells the police her nephew did it. But he wasn't the real killer. What happened?*

She read on for the answer.

But she didn't get past the next line. Even with

the television's volume down, the anchorwoman's voice seemed to boom across the room. With a start, Elizabeth looked up. "An arrest in yesterday's pharmacy holdup! Details right after these messages."

Dropping her book, Elizabeth sprinted to the stairs. "Jessica!" she shouted.

"I wonder who they arrested." Elizabeth's voice sounded calm, but inside she was shaking like a leaf. The commercials seemed to be taking forever.

"I hope it's somebody we hate," Jessica said, leaning closer.

The anchorwoman's face came back onto the screen. "Welcome back," she said with a toothy smile. "Last night the Sweet Valley Pharmacy was robbed at gunpoint by a man dressed as a clown. Today, Sweet Valley police have made an arrest. Our reporter has that story."

The video cut to a building that Elizabeth thought she recognized. "The Cute Little Kids Day-Care Center," a man's voice said ominously as the camera panned slowly up and down the building's entrance. "Today, the children enrolled in this program expected to see a clown act. Instead, they got this."

A police siren started blaring. "Get him!" Jessica shouted happily, grabbing a carrot stick. In the background, Elizabeth could see two uniformed police officers struggling with a man in a clown outfit—

An awfully familiar-looking clown outfit. Elizabeth drew in her breath. "Oh, man," she said softly.

"That's the guy, Lizzie!" Jessica bit into the carrot. "I'd know that costume anywhere. Remember that humongous button? And the fringe and—"

"Shh!" Elizabeth said quickly. She moved closer and turned up the volume a notch.

The reporter was speaking again. "But when he arrived at the day-care center, the police, acting on a tip, arrested him immediately."

"Good for them," Jessica said, gesturing with what was left of her carrot.

Elizabeth squeezed her hands together. *What had Joe said the other day? Something about performing his clown act for a—*

She felt her stomach clench.

For a day-care center!

On the screen, the clown was being forced roughly into the back of the police car. "He looks familiar, all right," Elizabeth said slowly, looking hard at the clown's piercing blue eyes. Her heart hammered in her chest.

"Of course he does." Jessica made an impatient noise. "He's the guy who robbed the store last night, silly."

"That's not what I meant." Elizabeth stared hard at the clown's face. She bit her lip. *The oversize shoes, the red-and-blue clown suit, the makeup applied so perfectly around the mouth—*

It all added up to only one thing. And Elizabeth didn't want to think about it.

The camera showed several children standing at the windows of the center. Two were crying. One held her arms out toward the clown. Another was being comforted by a teacher. "They all look so terribly sad," Elizabeth murmured. Her own eyes began to tear up.

"So who's the bad guy?" Jessica demanded, leaning forward in anticipation.

The anchorwoman's smiling face popped back up onto the television screen. "Police have only just now released the suspect's name. Here at Channel 37, we're proud to be the first to broadcast the news you need to know!"

"Get to the point," Jessica said, wolfing down another carrot stick.

Elizabeth's mouth felt dry. She stood up, swaying a little unsteadily on her feet as she stared at the television. *Don't say it!* she wanted to scream at the anchorwoman. *Don't ever say it! Let's just pretend this whole thing never happened—please?*

She didn't want to watch, but she didn't dare take her eyes off the screen, either.

The anchorwoman put on her most serious voice. "Arrested for the crime was a Sweet Valley resident, twenty-two-year-old Joseph Carrey."

"Not Joe!" Elizabeth swallowed hard. "Take it back!" she implored the anchorwoman. *Say it's all a joke! Say you didn't really mean it!*

"*Joe?*" A look of surprise crossed Jessica's face. "Wow! I guess—" Slowly she shook her head. "I guess you just never know."

"In other news—" The anchorwoman was speaking again, but Elizabeth wasn't listening any longer. Tears stung her eyes. *Not Joe! It just can't be Joe!*

Suddenly she couldn't bear to look at the anchorwoman anymore. Leaning forward, Elizabeth snapped the TV off with a savage flick of the wrist.

"Hey!" Jessica called indignantly, but Elizabeth had already bolted from the room.

Four

◇

"One strawberry milk shake, please," Elizabeth said softly on Saturday. It was after lunch, and she and some other kids were sitting at Casey's again.

Casey's with one important difference, she thought sadly.

The guy behind the counter!

"Strawberry?" Jeff Casey's mouth curled into a sneer. "You kidding me or something? Nobody drinks strawberry milk shakes. Nobody except little kids." He stared meaningfully at Elizabeth.

"He's right, Lizzie," Jessica hastened to add. "They've got lots of other flavors on the menu." She started ticking them off on her fingers. "They've got toasted banana almond crunch, and lemon-lime sorbet, and—"

"I *like* strawberry." Elizabeth gave her sister a

frosty stare, then turned back to Jeff. "A strawberry milk shake, please."

Jeff shrugged and rolled his eyes. "Coming right up," he muttered. Seizing a glass from the shelf, he spooned ice cream into it. Elizabeth's face fell. *Joe would have given me more*, she thought sorrowfully.

Mandy peered into her soda and frowned. "Hey, I ordered this one without nuts."

"Take 'em off, then," Jeff said, not looking up.

"But—," Mandy began. Then she shook her head. Reaching down into her glass, she began fishing out pieces of nut one by one.

"Could I have some more whipped cream?" Elizabeth thought Amy's voice sounded a little louder than usual. When Jeff didn't answer, Amy tried again. "Umm—Joe always put a little extra whipped cream on—"

Jeff snorted. "Get used to it, kid," he said. "What do you think this is, a charity? It's a *business*. I don't give things away." He picked up a wet dishrag and grazed it across the counter.

Elizabeth looked at a pool of melting chocolate ice cream he'd missed. *When Joe was here, the counter was always gleaming*, she thought. *Looks like Jeff didn't even bother to clean up from the last people who were here!*

"Isn't that amazing about Joe?" Mandy asked as she wiped her hands on her napkin. "I'm having a hard time believing it."

"I know what you mean." Maria shook her head.

"Well, believe it." Jeff slammed the milk shake down on the counter in front of Elizabeth. "I knew he was a loser the moment I laid eyes on him."

Elizabeth and Jessica exchanged glances. *No one asked you, Jeff,* Elizabeth found herself thinking. But she didn't dare say it aloud. She reached for her straw—and discovered that Jeff hadn't bothered to give her one. "Umm—could I have a straw, please?"

"Here." Jeff tossed her one without bothering to unwrap it.

"Thanks." Elizabeth decided to be polite anyway. She tore open the wrapper. "Do you think he's—he's going to be found guilty?" she asked, suspecting she knew what the answer would be.

"Darn right!" Jeff burst in.

"Oh, absolutely." Lila flashed her cat-that-ate-the-canary smile. "My father knows this guy who works for the sheriff's department," she announced, "and he says the case is, like, practically closed. It was definitely Joe."

Jessica shook her head. "Can you imagine?" she said, sipping her soda. "All this time, here we were, ordering ice cream from a robber! And we never even guessed." She gave a little shiver.

Elizabeth could feel a knot in her stomach. "Isn't there anybody who thinks he's innocent?" she asked, trying to keep her voice light.

"Innocent!" Jeff scoffed. "Don't make me laugh." He threw the cloth at the sink and disappeared into the back of the store.

"I don't really see how he could be." Maria turned to face Elizabeth. "All the evidence seems to point right at him. I mean, it was his clown suit, wasn't it? You saw it yourself."

"It was his clown suit, all right," Jessica confirmed before Elizabeth could respond. "Oh, hey, by the way, did I tell you how I almost tripped him?"

"Really?" Mandy raised her eyebrows.

"You didn't, either." Elizabeth felt tired. She set the straw right in the middle of her milk shake and watched it fall slowly to the side. *If Joe had made this shake,* she thought sadly, *it'd be so thick that the straw would stay perfectly upright. If Joe were still working here.* She sighed. "But the clown suit's all the evidence they've found, isn't it?" she asked hopefully.

"Not quite," Mandy said, spitting out a nut. "They haven't found the money or the weapon yet, but I heard that Joe says he was just sitting home that night. He *says,*" she added for emphasis. "But no one knows for sure."

"So he could have lied," Amy said thoughtfully. "He wasn't out with friends or anyone who could prove where he was."

"But—" Elizabeth felt as if she were swimming against the tide.

"And that's not all," Lila went on. "This guy at the sheriff's department—the one my dad knows? He says Joe needed money. Like, really, really bad." She frowned and shook her head, but there was a gleam in her eye. "My father says people will do very strange things to get money."

"I should have known," Jessica said abruptly. "I should have known he was guilty. He always acted kind of, you know, suspicious."

"Suspicious?" Elizabeth burst out. "Jessica, how can you say that? Suspicious like how?"

Jessica frowned. "Like, there was the way he always wore the same kind of clothes," she said, narrowing her eyes and leaning closer to her sister. "And the way he knew all those brainteasers."

Elizabeth couldn't believe her ears. "What's so suspicious about knowing brainteasers?" she demanded. "Since when is it a crime to tell people puzzles?"

"Well . . ." Jessica fingered her collar. "It isn't, I guess. But don't you think someone who knows lots of puzzles might also have, you know"—her gaze traveled from one girl to the next—"a criminal mind?"

"Uh-huh," Mandy said slowly. "That makes sense."

"And there's the way he's always so *nice*," Lila added, stabbing the air with her forefinger. "Remember how he gave me those extra cherries?"

"You're right, Lila," Jessica agreed. "He was too nice. Criminals always try to act real nice so you'll think they aren't really criminals."

Elizabeth stared in dismay, from Jessica to Lila and back. "But people are innocent until they're found guilty," she said, her voice not much more than a squeak. "In court! How can you say all these things about him? Joe hasn't been proven guilty."

"Yet," Mandy commented, shaking her head.

Elizabeth set her glass down on the counter with a clatter. "But what if he's not guilty at all?" she demanded. "Did you ever think of that?"

Lila sighed, fluttering her eyelashes as she did. "But if Joe is innocent, then why did the police arrest him?"

"Really, Elizabeth," Jessica chimed in. "Think about it."

"The police can make mistakes," Elizabeth said. She folded her arms firmly across her body. "And I think he's innocent."

Amy drew in her breath. "But, Elizabeth, all the evidence—"

"Who cares about the evidence?" Elizabeth broke in, her heart racing. "Joe is innocent, do you hear me?" She stared at the row of faces, all turned toward her. "And I'm going to prove it!"

"We're home!" Jessica hurried inside the Wakefields' house half an hour later, Elizabeth straggling along behind. "Hi, Mom! Hi, Dad! Hi— *oof!*" Turning a corner, she ran squarely into her brother, Steven.

"Why don't you watch where you're going, huh?" Steven snapped. Jessica stepped back quickly. Steven had a fully loaded plate in one hand. In the other, he held both a glass of milk and a dish of ice cream. "You could have destroyed my lunch!"

"Lunch?" Jessica looked curiously at the clock. *Two fifteen.* "Why are you eating lunch now instead of at noon like a normal human being?"

Steven shrugged. "See, this is actually my second lunch. Some of us don't believe in starvation, you know." He took a sip of milk, somehow managing not to spill the ice cream.

Jessica shook her head. "Starvation? Yeah, right!" Nudging Elizabeth, she watched a potato chip fall off Steven's plate and land on the floor. "Why don't you go sit down with that instead of messing up the whole entire kitchen?"

"I was about to," Steven said icily, "when some idiot came roaring into the house and bumped into me." Walking into the living room, he set his food down on the coffee table.

"What kind of sandwich is that, anyway?" Jessica asked.

"Peanut butter and salami." Steven reached for the dish of ice cream.

"Totally gross." Jessica wrinkled her nose.

"No one asked you," Steven pointed out. "And anyway I'm starting with this." He pointed to the ice cream. "Which reminds me of a brainteaser I just heard this morning. I got it right away, of course. There were two doctors and two grandmothers—" He paused to take a bite.

Jessica stole a quick glance at Elizabeth. Her sister seemed lost in thought.

"You all right, Lizzie?" she asked softly.

"Umm—yeah," Elizabeth said slowly. "It's just that brainteasers make me think of—well, make me think of Joe."

Jessica nodded. She felt kind of bad about ganging up on Joe at Casey's, especially because it obviously upset Elizabeth. But what could she do? All the evidence *did* point to Joe. Besides, she wanted to make sure that people kept focusing on the criminal. That way no one would wonder what she was doing in the pharmacy that evening.

"You listening or not?" Steven demanded. "And these guys, the doctors and the grandmothers, they went into—" He licked the spoon. "Into, umm, into—"

"Talk English, please," Jessica said sarcastically.

"Into a, you know, an ice cream parlor." He jabbed his spoon back into the dish. Out of the corner of her eye, Jessica could see Elizabeth stiffen. "And they ordered, let me see, umm—" He took another bite. "Boy, this stuff is really good. They each ordered one ice cream cone, OK? Then when the order comes, there's, umm—" Steven pulled the dish closer to him and dug to the bottom with his spoon.

"Never mind your ice cream!" Jessica suppressed an impulse to grab the dish and hide it till Steven finished the story. "Just tell us!"

"There's one chocolate cone," Steven went on, scooping up an extra-large spoonful and thrusting it into his mouth. "One vanilla." He stabbed a finger into the air and swallowed noisily. "And, umm, one strawberry. And that was it. But they didn't complain. How come?"

"Strawberry," Elizabeth sighed. She bit her lip. Sliding out of her chair, she headed for the stairs.

"Where are you going?" Jessica called after her.

"Don't you want to try to solve the puzzle?" Steven asked in surprise, trickles of ice cream pooling beneath his lower lip.

"Maybe later." Elizabeth smiled wanly. "I just don't want to think about . . . strawberry ice cream right now." She darted out of the living room.

"What's with her?" Steven jerked a thumb over his shoulder.

Jessica stared after her sister. "Strawberry ice cream reminds her of Joe Carrey," she explained, "and she's feeling kind of bad about Joe right now. She's positive that Joe didn't do the robbery the other night."

"Really?" Steven shook his head in disbelief. "But if the police arrested him—"

"I know what you're saying," Jessica told him with a sigh. "I really wish it wasn't him, too. But all the evidence points to him. I mean, it was Joe's clown suit and everything. Elizabeth even saw it!"

And even though I don't want Joe to be guilty, she told herself, *it's better to have the case closed. Otherwise, people might start to wonder why I went to the pharmacy that night!*

"Oh, that's right, you guys were there, weren't

you?" Steven sat up a little straighter. "I forgot. What was it you went there to buy?"

Jessica peered at her brother. *He looks perfectly innocent*, she told herself. *But I'm not about to take any chances!*

"Oh—something," she said vaguely, flashing him her friendliest smile. "I forget exactly what."

"Christine's fingers spun the telephone dial. As she waited for the police force to answer her call, she thought over what she would say."

"Good for you, Christine," Elizabeth mumbled into the bedclothes. Down in the living room, she could dimly hear Jessica trying to guess the solution to Steven's brainteaser. She tried hard not to think about strawberry ice cream—or poor Joe Carrey. Sighing, she focused on the book in her hand.

"Of course, Jay couldn't possibly have played a role in his aunt's death, Christine told herself. No matter what evidence there was against him, there must be some other explanation.

"'River City police.' The voice sounded weary.

"Christine gripped the phone. 'Yes,' she said in a steely voice. 'I must speak to the detective in charge of the Jay Carroll case—immediately.'

"'I'm afraid that's impossible,' came the reply.

"'Nothing is impossible.' Christine drew herself up to her full height. 'I demand to speak to the detective right away, or else I shall have to inform your supervisor. The force has made a serious mistake. Did I make

it clear that my name is Christine Davenport?'

"*'Ah.' There was a scuffling noise, and suddenly a new voice came on the line. 'Detective Scott here, Miss Davenport. How may I help you?'*"

Elizabeth sighed and shook her head. Christine was always so good at getting what she wanted—

Hey.

A little light went on in Elizabeth's mind. "I could do that," she said half to herself. "I could call the detectives who are handling Joe's case, just like Christine's doing!"

The thought made her suddenly happier. Jumping up from her bed, she padded down the stairs in search of the telephone directory. *If Christine can do it, so can I!* she told herself, beginning to plan what she would say. *"This is Elizabeth Wakefield. I demand to speak to the detective in charge of the Joe Carrey case—"*

Feeling a surge of hope, Elizabeth realized there was something she had to do first.

"Hey, Steven!" she called, popping into the living room, where her brother was devouring the last few crumbs of his sandwich. "About that brainteaser? When they only got three cones, no one complained because there were only three people in all!"

Jessica gave her sister a disapproving look. "Come on, Lizzie, that's not helpful. We already know there were four—two grandmothers, two doctors." She patted the place beside her on the couch. "And the answer isn't that one of the grand-mothers died after they ordered. I already guessed that one."

"But there *were* only three." For the first time in what seemed like days, Elizabeth couldn't hold back a smile. "Didn't it ever occur to you that a grandmother could be a doctor, too?"

Five

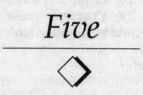

"Sweet Valley police," a perky voice said. "How may I direct your call?"

"Umm . . ." Elizabeth bit her lip. She couldn't imagine how Christine Davenport managed to be so—so forceful. "I'd like to speak to the detective in charge of the Joe Carrey case. Please. If it isn't too much trouble," she added hastily just in case the receptionist decided to hang up on her.

"One moment." There was a buzz and a click. Then there was silence. After a few seconds, music began to play.

"Wow!" Elizabeth said aloud. *I can't believe I'll get to talk to the detective on the first try!* Drumming her fingers nervously, Elizabeth leaned against the kitchen counter to wait.

* * *

"Sweet Valley police."

There she is again, Elizabeth thought miserably. *What is this, the sixth time I've talked to her?* "I just wanted to talk to—"

"Oh yes," the voice interrupted, sounding just as perky as ever. "It's this terrible new phone system. We just keep cutting you off, don't we! Now, you wanted to talk to the detective in charge of the Corey case, right?"

"The Carrey case," Elizabeth said desperately. "It's a matter of life and death!"

"Let me try this button," the woman said perkily. "Hang on."

There was a click and a buzz. "Hello?" Elizabeth said into the receiver. But no one replied.

The line was dead.

"Sweet Valley police."

"Please!" Elizabeth began, clutching the phone as tightly as she could. *How much more of this can I take?* "I really, really need to talk to—"

"The detective in charge of the Currie case." The receptionist's voice sounded even perkier than before. "Let me try this button."

Elizabeth could hear what sounded like the ringing of a phone. There was a click. "Hello?" she said eagerly. "Hello, this—"

"You have reached the Sweet Valley police," a metallic voice interrupted her. "All circuits are presently in use. If this is an emergency and you know your area code, please press "one" now. If this is not an emergency and your last name begins with A through F, please press—"

Elizabeth stared at the phone in her hand. *An answering machine*, she thought bitterly.

Why didn't this ever happen to Christine Davenport?

"Detective Holmes here."

Elizabeth breathed deeply. "Umm—you're a real person, aren't you?" she asked slowly. "Not an answering machine or anything?"

"So they tell me." There was a tearing noise in the background. "What do you want, kid? I haven't got all day."

Elizabeth bit her lip. All the brave, forceful things she'd been planning to say had suddenly flown away, now that she'd finally reached the detective. "Umm—I wanted to ask you some questions about the, umm, the Joe Carrey case," she said, her voice catching on the last few words.

"The what?" There was a munching sound, as though Detective Holmes were eating a candy bar. "You got to speak up, kid." *Munch, munch.*

"The Joe Carrey case." Elizabeth hung on to the receiver for dear life. "Joe Carrey. Remember? The guy you thought robbed a pharmacy a couple of days ago?"

The detective swallowed. "You mean, the guy who *did* rob the pharmacy. What about him?"

Elizabeth thought hard. The conversation wasn't

going the way she'd hoped. "You see—officer—the thing is, you made a mistake."

"A mistake, huh?" *Chomp. Munch.* Elizabeth squeezed her eyelids shut. Detective Holmes didn't seem to be taking her very seriously. "Who is this, anyway?"

"My name is Elizabeth Wakefield," Elizabeth said loudly, remembering what had happened in the book when Christine Davenport had told the police who she was.

Munch. Munch. "Well, nice to know you, Miss Wickfield. And why do you think we've made a mistake here?" Detective Holmes asked through the candy bar.

Elizabeth felt herself turning red. "Umm—I know Joe Carrey, like, really well, and he's this really, really nice guy—"

Detective Holmes snorted. "Listen, sister, if I had a dime for every 'nice guy' I've arrested, I'd—" In the background Elizabeth could hear the tearing of another candy bar wrapper. "He might be nice. He's also a robber. Trust me." *Chomp.*

Elizabeth tried to hold firm. "Did you find the gun?" she asked, afraid the detective would hang up. "Did you find the money?"

"Did *you* find any evidence that he didn't do it?" Detective Holmes spoke with his mouth full of candy bar.

"Umm—well, not exactly." Elizabeth stared at the floor.

The detective laughed. "Listen, kid," he said. *Munch, munch.* "Don't call us." *Chomp, munch, swallow.* "We'll call you."

"If at first you don't succeed, try again," Elizabeth told herself a few minutes later. Even though Detective Holmes hadn't listened to her at all, Elizabeth wasn't ready to give up. In her mystery novel, Christine was talking to everyone who knew Jay, hoping to find clues that would prove her friend was innocent. Elizabeth was determined to do the same thing.

She grabbed a pink sweater from the floor of her room, wondering why she hadn't bothered to put it away. Then she shivered. The sweater was the same one that Jessica had borrowed a couple of days before, the sweater her sister had worn to the pharmacy.

Elizabeth's fingers traced the EW monogram on the front. Then she shook her head and put the sweater on, trying not to think about that terrible evening.

"I loved that boy like a son." Old Mr. Casey looked ready to cry.

Elizabeth nodded. She and Mr. Casey were sitting at a table in the almost empty ice cream parlor. Nearby, Jeff scowled as he folded place mats, his blue eyes flashing angrily at Elizabeth. "I know how you feel, Mr. Casey," Elizabeth said softly.

"Do you?" Shaking his head, Mr. Casey twisted his hands together. "I don't know much about Joe's background, but I would have trusted him with anything. With my car, with my keys, with my store—" His mouth curled downward. "I was planning to turn the whole place over to him when I retired, you know," he added. "But now, I guess—"

Elizabeth bit her lip. Old Mr. Casey's eyes were brimming with tears.

"I guess you just can't always trust your instincts about people." Mr. Casey spoke in a gruff voice and fished a handkerchief out from his shirt pocket. "I wish he'd told me he needed money. I could have helped him, could have given him a loan . . ." His voice trailed off.

"So you think he did it." Elizabeth watched as Mr. Casey wiped his eyes.

Mr. Casey shook his head. "I hate to believe it, but I just can't figure out any other explanation. The clown suit was his. You saw it yourself, didn't you? The silly wig, the brown shoes with the letters on them. All that stuff."

Elizabeth's mind flashed back to Steven's brainteaser. *Four people really turn out to be three—* "Sometimes things seem impossible to explain," she said slowly. "But it turns out there's an easy answer. Once you think about it in a different way."

Mr. Casey sighed and ran his hand through his thinning hair. "I wish I could believe that."

*   *   *

Why am I doing this, anyway?

Elizabeth stood in front of the Sweet Valley University library, wondering whether she ought to go inside—or whether she should just go home. "After all, I'm the only person in the whole world who seems to think Joe's innocent," she said aloud. *My friends think he's guilty. The police think he's guilty. My own sister thinks he's guilty.* She sighed. *Even old Mr. Casey thinks he's guilty. So why am I bothering?*

Squinting in the late afternoon light, she looked up at the gray stone building in front of her. "Because I *know* he's innocent," she answered herself. "And if I don't prove it, who will?"

Squaring her shoulders, she walked into the library. A young woman at the front desk put down a newspaper and smiled at Elizabeth. "May I help you?" she asked.

"Maybe you can," Elizabeth said, smiling back. "I'm looking for someone who knows Joe Carrey."

"Joe Carrey." The young woman tapped the paper in front of her and shook her head. "What a sad business. I wouldn't have thought Joe would turn out to be a crook."

A surge of excitement rushed through Elizabeth's body. "So you knew him?"

"Not very well," the young woman replied. "Probably about as well as most people here, though. Why do you want to know?"

What would Christine Davenport say? Elizabeth wondered. *She'd tell the truth,* she decided. "I'm—

I'm kind of a friend of his," she said, swallowing hard to overcome her nervousness. "I don't think he's guilty, and I want to find out more about him."

The woman frowned. "I don't know how much I can tell you," she said. "But he was a nice guy. We sat together in class a couple of years back, and I got to know him a little then."

"Oh, you're a student here," Elizabeth asked with surprise. "I thought you were the librarian."

The woman smiled. "I work here for some extra money, that's all. My name's Wendy. What exactly do you want to know?"

"Oh—I'm not sure," Elizabeth said shyly. "Just—anything, I guess." She coughed. "I don't really know what I'm looking for."

Wendy shrugged. "Well, Joe was kind of a character, back when I first met him."

A character. That sounded promising. "What kind of character?" Elizabeth asked.

"For one thing, he used to buzz around the campus on this big blue motorcycle," Wendy told her, smiling at the memory. "You could hear it coming half a mile away. We'd hear *'Bang! Bang! Whiz!'* and we'd go, there's Joe on his bike." She shook her head. "That thing made a noise like you wouldn't believe."

Elizabeth grinned. "I've never seen him on a motorcycle," she admitted. She thought back. It seemed like Joe walked everywhere he went.

"He'd wear these surfer shorts, too," Wendy

went on. "Wore them everywhere he went—on the motorcycle, to class, to track practice—"

"He was on the track team?" Elizabeth asked, raising her eyebrows.

"Was he ever!" Wendy shook her head. "The guy could *run*. He had a full track scholarship, captain of the team, all-around good guy. And then . . ." She paused.

"And then what?" Elizabeth asked curiously. A million questions whirled through her mind. *Where's the motorcycle? What happened to those surfer shorts?* And most confusing of all, *If Joe is at college on a track scholarship, how come he has to work two jobs?*

"Hmm." Wendy rubbed her nose thoughtfully. "Then came summer break. And when we got back in the fall, Joe wasn't there. He'd dropped out."

"Dropped out?" Elizabeth stared at Wendy. "But—but why?"

Wendy shrugged. "I don't know," she said. "And I don't think anyone around here does. He just plain disappeared."

Elizabeth's mouth felt dry. "But he came back."

"Uh-huh." Wendy nodded. "After, oh, about a year. He gave up his scholarship, he quit track. He got a couple of jobs—" She frowned. "One was mowing lawns and the other was, like, working in a pizza parlor or something."

"Ice cream parlor," Elizabeth corrected her. "Casey's."

"Ice cream, that's right." Wendy stretched out her arms. "And that's really all I know about him."

Elizabeth shook her head. Somehow the more information she had, the less she understood.

Six

◇

"Steven?"

Groaning, Steven turned over in his bed and peered at the clock. *Too early,* he thought grumpily. "Who's that?" he grumbled.

"It's Elizabeth," a voice said from the hallway. "Could I come in?"

"Come *in*?" Steven struggled to a sitting position. "Elizabeth, in case you don't know, it's incredibly early in the morning. Come back in, oh, about three hours." He slammed his pillow onto the bed. "On second thought, make it four."

"Oh." Elizabeth's voice sounded disappointed. "But I've got a new brainteaser for you."

A new brainteaser? Tired as he was, Steven felt a tiny bit curious. "Well—umm—couldn't it wait a little longer? Like, an hour or so?"

"Not really," Elizabeth said brightly. "I've got some errands to run. Fifteen minutes, tops."

Fifteen minutes? Steven hesitated. *It's too early to breathe,* he told himself, *let alone try to solve a brainteaser. On the other hand—*

On the other hand, he didn't want to miss out on the brainteaser. Elizabeth had told him some halfway decent ones before.

"How about twenty minutes?" he called, emerging from the covers.

"Twenty minutes," Elizabeth agreed.

"OK, shoot." Steven leaned forward in his chair at the breakfast table and shoveled a spoonful of cereal into his mouth.

Elizabeth grinned. It had been twenty minutes exactly since she'd knocked on her brother's door. "All right," she began. "There was this guy who went to college. He was a track star, and he had a full scholarship."

"Track star," Steven said around another mouthful of cereal. "Got it."

"Then he disappeared for a year," Elizabeth went on, "a whole year, and no one knew what had happened to him."

"Huh," Steven said dismissively. He grabbed the pitcher of juice and poured a glass.

"And when he came back," Elizabeth added, "he'd quit the track team, and he'd given up his scholarship."

"Stupid idiot!" Steven said.

"Maybe." Elizabeth spread out her hands. "The question is, why? What happened?"

"Well." Steven slurped down a few soggy grains of cereal and pushed his bowl away. "There has to be a reasonable explanation."

Elizabeth looked at him intently. "Yeah. But what?"

"The first thing to do is to narrow down the possibilities," Steven went on as if Elizabeth hadn't spoken. "That's what a detective would do. So, let's see." He narrowed his eyes and wiggled his spoon between his fingers. "All right, then. Did he owe somebody a lot of money? Like on credit cards?"

Elizabeth frowned. "Why would that make him give up his scholarship?"

Steven raised his eyebrows. "He wouldn't on purpose. But certain people might want to make him, you know, disappear if he owed them too much money."

Elizabeth frowned. "I don't see—"

"Well, when you get to be my age you'll understand," Steven said quickly. "So did he owe tons of money?"

"Umm—I don't know," Elizabeth replied honestly.

"Doesn't matter, huh?" Steven rubbed his forehead. "OK. How's this? Maybe the guy was a spy for some foreign power."

Elizabeth wrinkled her nose. It was hard to imagine Joe as a spy in disguise. "I don't think—"

"No? OK. Hmm." Steven strummed his fingers

on the table. "You said he was on the track team?"

At last, a question I can answer. "Yes," Elizabeth said, nodding.

"Then it's simple." Steven grinned hugely and leaned back in his chair. "He was stealing track equipment from the college and selling it. Then they caught him and kicked him out."

Track equipment? Elizabeth bit her lip. "What kind of track equipment is worth stealing?"

Steven's eyes twinkled. "You'd be surprised. High jump bars. Stopwatches. Umm—those big metal balls you throw, you know, shot puts."

"And you can make a lot of money from that?" Elizabeth asked skeptically.

"Oh, sure." Steven picked up the rest of his orange juice and downed it in one gulp. "The really top college programs would pay anything for stuff like that."

"Really?" Elizabeth pushed a stray piece of hair from her eyes. "Why don't they just buy the stuff from the companies that make it, then?"

"Because!" Steven tossed his napkin in the air. "Look, take my word for it, they just do. It's cheaper, all right? So was this guy stealing track equipment?"

"Umm . . ." Elizabeth hesitated. "I don't know. I don't think so."

"Oh, for crying out loud!" Steven looked at Elizabeth as though he wanted to jump down her throat. With a bang, he set his glass back on the table.

"OK. Did he have any friends on the track team?"

Elizabeth took a deep breath. "I don't really know."

Steven rolled his eyes. "All *right*," he snapped. "How about this. Did he leave the country the year he disappeared?"

"I don't know that either," Elizabeth admitted in a small voice. Somehow, this wasn't going exactly the way she'd planned.

"Well, what *do* you know?" Steven asked with frustration. "Do you even know the answer?"

Slowly, Elizabeth shook her head. "That's exactly the problem," she said sadly. "I hoped you would figure it out—because I don't have a clue!"

"I still think you're crazy." Jessica stepped off the bus a few hours later, following just behind Elizabeth. She gestured at the sign in front of them. "'Sweet Valley Jail,'" she read aloud. "They'll never let us in there to talk to Joe. And even if by some bizarre chance they do, what are you planning to say, anyway?"

Elizabeth's mouth was a determined line. "I think I can get us in," she said. "And as for the other part—well, I want Joe to know that we're on his side."

We? Jessica rolled her eyes, but she decided not to say anything. *I don't know why I ever let you talk me into this!*

"Also, I want to ask him why he quit the track team," Elizabeth went on. "I just have this hunch that I could solve the whole puzzle if only I knew why." She shook her head and pushed open the massive door marked VISITORS.

Jessica sighed deeply. "Maybe he just got tired of running all the time. I know I would."

"Yeah, but—," Elizabeth broke off and pointed to a desk at the end of the hall. "I guess we go over there."

"I guess." Jessica looked around timidly as she followed Elizabeth to the desk. The hallway seemed awfully quiet and dark. The walls were painted an ugly tan-gray color, and the girls' footsteps echoed ominously. "'Visitors only from ten to twelve weekday mornings,'" Jessica read. "Is it past noon yet?" she asked Elizabeth hopefully.

"Not yet." Elizabeth didn't look at her sister.

Jessica frowned. She wished she hadn't agreed to come along with Elizabeth.

"May I help you?" A tall woman in a uniform stood up from her seat.

"Umm—yes." Elizabeth's voice sounded very small in the enormous hallway. "We were wondering if we—if we could see"—she licked her lip nervously—"if we could see Joe Carrey," she finished in one quick burst.

"Carrey?" The woman frowned. "Do you spell that with a K?"

"C," Elizabeth corrected her. "Please."

Jessica watched the woman drop back into her chair. "Carrey, Carrey," she muttered, punching some buttons on a small computer terminal. "Carrey with a C—here we go." She looked dubiously at the twins. "He's in for armed robbery," she said.

"I know." Elizabeth swallowed hard.

"And the case hasn't come to trial yet. That means only relatives are allowed to visit. You relatives?" Her eyes darted from Elizabeth to Jessica and back.

"I knew we should never have come," Jessica hissed, turning around. She wouldn't be sorry to leave this spooky old place.

"Shh!" Elizabeth gave her a dirty look. Turning back to the guard and changing her expression to a smile, she spoke loudly. "Yes, we're relatives."

"We are?" Jessica felt a jolt of surprise. Her sister never lied about anything.

Elizabeth laughed lightly. "Of *course* we're relatives!" she said, carefully separating every word. "Aren't we, Jess?"

"But—," Jessica began. Then all at once she understood. *Yeah, we're relatives, all right,* she told herself. *We're not Joe's relatives, but we're relatives.*

"Relatives," Elizabeth repeated, glaring icily at Jessica.

Jessica reluctantly met her twin's eyes. "Right. We're relatives," she agreed at last. *Pretty cute, Lizzie,* she thought. Even though she didn't want to go into the jail at all, she had to hand it to her sister.

The guard shrugged. "This way, please," she

said, standing up and taking an enormous key from the wall in front of her.

Elizabeth gave Jessica a thumbs-up signal. "We're in!" she whispered happily behind the guard's back.

"This room is pretty disgusting," Jessica said, wrinkling her nose. The two girls sat in the middle of the visiting room, on one side of a wire screen that separated the prisoners from the visitors.

Elizabeth nodded sadly. "It's—awful." The room was hot and full of flies. A tired old ceiling fan turned slowly above her head. At one end of the room, a woman and a very small child leaned toward the screen. Elizabeth could see tears trickling down the child's cheeks.

"Oh, here he comes." Jessica stared off through the wire screen. "Boy, he looks terrible."

"Jessica!" Elizabeth glared at her sister.

"Well, he does!" Jessica pointed at the approaching figure.

Elizabeth turned to see. She had to admit, Joe *did* look pretty bad. Shuffling along, wrists cuffed firmly together, Joe was staring at the ground. The white T-shirt and black pants were gone, replaced by a prison outfit that looked like a pair of pajamas. The shirt was too big, and the pants hung down way over his shoes. But worst of all, it looked to Elizabeth as if all the life had gone out of Joe's bright blue eyes.

It's like a mask, she thought, drawing in her breath. *It's like he's wearing a mask!*

"Ten minutes," the guard said as Joe took his seat on the other side of the screen.

"Hi there," he said hollowly. The corners of his lips turned upward in a weak smile. "Well—I'm glad you came."

"Oh, Joe." Elizabeth suddenly didn't know what to say. She longed to reach out and take his hand, but she couldn't reach through the screen. "Umm—" She swallowed. "I wanted to tell you that we're behind you. I know you didn't do it."

Joe's lip quivered and he looked sadly down at his hands.

Elizabeth licked her lips. Above her, the fan spun slowly. "We—we all miss you. At Casey's, I mean."

Joe nodded. His face looked pinched, as though he hadn't slept much. "I hope Jeff is treating you well."

"Jeff!" Jessica scoffed. "Give me a break! You know how many sprinkles he gave me on my cone yesterday?"

A fly landed on Joe's elbow, but he didn't make a motion to brush it off. "Jeff's not one to give things away if he can charge money for them."

Elizabeth drummed her fingers anxiously on the arm of her chair. She could hear the child at the other end of the room beginning to wail. And she couldn't hold herself back any longer. "Joe," she burst out, "why did you quit the track team?"

For the first time during the visit, Joe looked directly at Elizabeth. "I beg your pardon?"

Elizabeth pressed her hand to her cheek. *Is being a detective always so embarrassing?* she wondered. But she'd already asked the question. It would be too hard to pretend she hadn't. "Please, Joe," she said softly, leaning forward. "I—I need to know why you quit the track team in college."

Joe sat back with a faint sigh. "Oh, Elizabeth," he said sadly, "I don't want to talk about that."

Elizabeth looked at him pleadingly. "But Joe—"

Joe gave a slight shake of his head.

Elizabeth bit her lip and gazed around the dingy room: the peeling paint, the battered fan, the flies buzzing near the windows. "All right," she said at last. "But I want you to know that I'm positive you're innocent. And I'm going to get you out of here." She squeezed her hands together. "And that's a promise!"

There really isn't any evidence besides the clown suit, Elizabeth thought. The twins had just gotten home, and Elizabeth was sprawled out on her bed, trying as hard as she could to be hopeful. Still, she couldn't forget Joe's awful, blank, masklike face.

With a sigh, Elizabeth picked up her mystery book from the floor and found her place. She had to get her mind off Joe, for just a little while anyway.

" 'So you're Jay's cousin.' *Christine looked quickly up and down the young man in front of her.*

"'Yeah, that's me—Chauncey Bleecker.' The man laughed loudly and clapped Christine on the back. 'So ol' Jay's got himself put in jail for killing Aunt Susan, huh? Didn't know he had it in him!' Bleecker laughed again, revealing uneven yellowish teeth.

"'Some of us believe in innocent until proven guilty,' Christine replied, making no attempt to conceal her distaste for the man.

"'Sure, sure.' Bleecker waved his hand in the air. 'I gotta say, kid, I hope they get him. Ya know why?' He winked at Christine. ''Cause if he's found guilty, I get Aunt Susan's whole estate!'

"'You do?' Christine asked curiously.

"'Darn right.' Bleecker headed for the door. 'Be seeing you, toots!' he yelled over his shoulder.

"For a moment Christine stood still. Then she made up her mind. Grabbing her handbag, she strode out the door, keeping a careful distance behind Bleecker.

"I'm going to follow him! *she thought.*"

Eyes blazing, Elizabeth sat up. The book fell out of her hands and crashed to the floor, but she didn't care.

"It's just like what's happening to Joe!" she said aloud. "I bet Bleecker killed Aunt Susan and made it look like it was Jay—just so he could get her estate! Maybe someone else robbed the pharmacy and is trying to frame Joe—someone who . . ."

Her voice trailed off. *Someone who will benefit if Joe is found guilty,* she thought. She wrinkled her nose. *Who?*

All of a sudden she could hear Mr. Casey's voice echoing in her head. *"I was planning to turn the whole place over to Joe when I retired, you know."*

Then a picture came into her mind: Jeff Casey, snarling at Joe. *"This store doesn't belong to you. Yet!"*

Elizabeth clapped her hand over her mouth. "Oh!" she gasped. "If Joe doesn't inherit the store, then—"

Then I bet Mr. Casey will give it to Jeff!

Grabbing a sweater, Elizabeth dashed out of the house, heading for Casey's.

She had a little spying of her own to do!

Seven

"You going to buy anything else?" Jeff Casey demanded. "Or are you just going to sit there all day?"

Elizabeth held up the remains of her root beer. "Umm—I'm not quite done with this one yet," she said weakly. "Thanks."

Jeff sneered. "Bet there's nothing in there but ice!"

"No, there's some root beer left," Elizabeth insisted. She took a quick gulp of the liquid at the bottom. *Yuck,* she thought, making a face as the melted ice went down her throat. *I can't even tell if this used to be root beer or orange pop!* "Plenty of root beer left," she said aloud, crossing her fingers beneath the table as Jeff rolled his eyes.

When Jeff went to wait on another customer, Elizabeth checked her watch. Two o'clock. She'd been sitting there for just over an hour. *Of course, it seems like six*, she thought gloomily, forcing herself to watch Jeff as he threw a sundae together behind the counter. *I don't care what Christine Davenport says, spying is very boring work.*

If only Jeff would do something—something suspicious.

Elizabeth stirred the remains of her drink with her straw and considered what she'd seen. In the last hour, Jeff had made exactly seven sundaes, three ice cream sodas, and eight ice cream cones, two of them double scoop. Somehow, she couldn't imagine how any of that could be important information. He'd stopped once to make a telephone call—Elizabeth could see into the back room where the phone hung on the wall—and he'd made one trip through a brown door behind the telephone. *Not exactly suspicious!* she figured.

Elizabeth popped an ice cube into her mouth and sucked on it. A few minutes ago, Jeff had used an ice cream scoop twice without bothering to rinse it off in between. *But that doesn't count as a crime*, Elizabeth reminded herself, shaking her head.

The door opened. A boy and girl a few years older than Elizabeth came in timidly and approached the counter. *Johnny Gordon and Melanie Northrop*, Elizabeth thought, recognizing them as classmates of her brother's.

"Help you?" Jeff barked.

Johnny spoke first. "This the place where that Joe Carrey guy was working?" he asked. Beside him, Melanie leaned closer to the counter.

"You mean Joe Carrey-the-money-away?" Jeff's lips twisted into a tight grin. "Joe knows theft!" he chanted in a silly voice. "Joe knows clown suits! Joe knows getting caught!"

"Yeah, him." Johnny's face lit up. "What's he like, huh? We want to get, you know, the inside scoop on the guy."

"Well, you've come to the right place." Jeff set down the dishcloth in his hand and propped his elbows on the counter. "The guy's a total loser. I knew that the minute my uncle hired him."

What a jerk! Elizabeth thought, her eyes blazing. She wished she could run across the room and tell the teenagers the *real* truth about Joe. But she knew that Christine Davenport would never do anything like that, so she stayed where she was.

And even if Jeff's a jerk, she thought, wrinkling her nose in disgust, *there's no law against being a jerk!*

"Casey's. Jeff speaking. Who's this?"

Elizabeth sighed and stretched as Jeff answered the phone in the back room. Another half hour had gone by. She didn't know how much more of this she could take. She couldn't remember the last time she'd been so completely, totally bored.

Drumming her fingers on the counter, she stared into what was left of her root beer. *Two ice cubes,* she thought miserably, hoping they wouldn't melt quickly. She really didn't feel like ordering anything else.

"Uh-huh." Jeff's voice rang out clearly from the back room. Elizabeth sat up. She wished she could hear what was being said on the other end of the line. *It's probably no one very important, but you never know.*

Jeff turned his back.

Christine would find a way to listen in, Elizabeth thought, trying hard to pick out snatches of what Jeff was saying. *Maybe there's an extension. Or maybe I should try to get closer.* She was starting to ease out of her seat when suddenly the door of the ice cream parlor opened.

With a guilty start, Elizabeth sank back into her chair. "Some detective I am!" she whispered to herself. Her heart was pounding furiously. *How come Christine Davenport is never afraid of getting caught?*

She fidgeted with her napkin as Mr. Casey came into the room, looking even older and sadder than he had yesterday. When he saw Elizabeth, he smiled, but somehow it didn't seem like a real smile. "How are you?" Then he walked toward the back, not waiting for an answer.

Elizabeth could see Jeff spin around. "Talk to you later, then," he said into the phone. Then he slammed down the receiver. "Hey, Uncle Martin, can I knock off work for a while now?" he demanded, loosening his apron and taking off his cap.

Uncle Martin? Elizabeth frowned. *Oh, of course. He's Mr. Casey's nephew!* She shook her head. It was funny to think of Mr. Casey actually having a first name.

"All right." Mr. Casey waved a tired arm in

Jeff's direction. "Just be back by, I don't know, six."

"Sure, sure." With a quick motion, Jeff tossed his apron onto the floor. "Catch you then!" He made a dash for the exit.

Mr. Casey opened his mouth as if to say something. Then he shut it again. Sighing, he leaned down to pick up the apron. Elizabeth could see his knees swaying unsteadily as he braced himself against the counter. She wished she could take a couple of minutes to help him.

But if she was going to be a real spy, she knew she couldn't.

Sliding out of her seat, she rushed to the door—already ten seconds behind Jeff.

It's a good thing he isn't looking behind him, Elizabeth told herself a few minutes later. *He'd see me for sure!*

Jeff took a right turn at the next corner. Elizabeth let him get almost halfway down the block, then she sauntered across the intersection herself. She wished there were more people on the sidewalks. That way she might have someone to hide behind.

Jeff slowed to a stop. Putting his hands on his hips, he looked up at the sky.

He's going to look this way, Elizabeth thought. Her heart began to pound in her chest. Her eyes flickered left and right, searching for a place to hide. *I can't let him see me!* There was a streetlight, a parked car, and—

A doorway. Taking three quick steps, Elizabeth darted into an empty space near the entrance to a flower store. Kneeling, she peered carefully around the wall. Jeff was still staring up above his head. Elizabeth's eyes followed his. Her fingers curled together. *Is he doing something suspicious, at last?* she thought hopefully. Lifting her eyes farther up, she found herself looking straight at—

A hot-air balloon.

A hot-air balloon. Just great! Elizabeth thought grumpily, beginning to straighten up. *Nothing suspicious at all.* She stole an anxious glance at the sidewalk ahead of her. His hands in his pockets, Jeff was walking once again.

The door to the flower store swung open suddenly, hitting Elizabeth squarely in the side. "Ow!" she yelped, wincing with pain. Looking up, she saw an elderly lady with a bright yellow hat staring indignantly at her.

"Really, now. Is this a sensible place to play hide-and-seek?" the lady demanded.

Two blocks later, Elizabeth was about to give up hope. Jeff certainly wasn't acting like a man who was hiding something. He walked steadily forward, not bothering to skulk around in doorways and behind parked cars the way a criminal would.

The way a criminal would. Elizabeth shook her head. *Of course,* she said to herself, *it's not like I've known lots of criminals in my life. Maybe this is the way criminals really do walk.*

Ahead of her, Jeff stopped next to a three-story building. Fishing in his pocket, he pulled something out. Elizabeth strained to see. *Something small,* she said to herself. *Something that fits in his palm.*

She leaned closer. Light glinted off the object in Jeff's hand.

Something metal. For a moment Elizabeth stopped breathing. *A gun? It could be!* She almost wished it was—as long as Jeff wasn't going to aim it at her.

Then Elizabeth heard a jingle—and she let out her breath. *Just keys.*

Jeff darted inside the building and slammed the door shut behind him. Elizabeth forced herself to wait a few seconds before moving. Then, stepping slowly toward the door, Elizabeth leaned forward to read the names next to the buzzers on the intercom system. *Maybe he's breaking in,* she told herself hopefully. *Maybe he doesn't live here at all. Maybe he's upstairs in some poor guy's apartment right now, stealing all the electronic equipment.*

She drew in her breath. *Or maybe it's Joe's apartment,* she thought with a sudden shiver of excitement. *Maybe Jeff's gotten a key to Joe's apartment somehow, and while Joe's in jail, Jeff's going to—*

Her eyes locked on to the buzzer at the top right corner.

"Jeff Casey," she read sadly.

Another great idea bites the dust!

In broad daylight, the pharmacy looked a lot different to Elizabeth than it had during the holdup a few nights ago. Much more—ordinary, Elizabeth decided.

Too ordinary, in fact. There wasn't anything in sight that looked like a clue.

Of course, what did I expect? Elizabeth thought, sitting down on the curb in front of the store. *Size-22 clown shoes just kind of lying in the gutter? Some leftover cash strewn across the pavement, with Jeff's fingerprints all over it?* She rubbed her legs. "What I really want," she mumbled to no one in particular, "is a billboard. A humongous billboard that says, 'I was the robber! Signed, Jeff Casey.' And that's not going to happen."

"What's not going to happen?"

Startled, Elizabeth turned around. Amy Sutton stood there, a big grin on her face. "Hi, Amy," Elizabeth said, feeling a little embarrassed. "What are you doing here?"

"Going to Casey's," Amy replied promptly. "Want to come?"

"Well—" Elizabeth hesitated. It seemed like hours since she'd had that root beer. And she *was* starting to talk to herself—maybe that was a sign that she needed company.

"Oh, come on," Amy pressed her. "A double-scoop chocolate swirl and strawberry cone with sprinkles?"

Elizabeth smiled. Detective work could wait, she decided. "Ice cream sodas, I think," she said, taking Amy's arm. "Let's go!"

"Oh, I heard a new brainteaser last night," Amy said as the girls sipped their sodas at Casey's.

"Tell," Elizabeth commanded, wondering whether to let her ice cream scoops melt slowly into the soda or attack them with a spoon.

"There were these two brothers, Ray and Clay," Amy said, "and they were identical twins. There were only two tiny differences in their looks." She paused to sip her soda.

"And those differences were?" Elizabeth prompted her.

"One,"—Amy held up a finger—"Ray had a bald spot on top of his head. And two, Clay had a bright red birthmark that covered three fingers on his left hand."

Elizabeth nodded slowly. "OK."

"One day their mom came to see them do something, though." Turning her stool to face Elizabeth, Amy accidentally kicked her friend in the shin. Elizabeth winced. "Sorry! Anyway, when their mom comes to watch them that day, she can't tell which one is Clay and which one is Ray. Why not?"

Elizabeth smiled. "Could their mom see?"

"Uh-huh," Amy replied with a grin. "It's not

that easy. It took me a long time to figure out."

Thoughtfully, Elizabeth sipped her soda. "Was it light out?"

Amy nodded. "Plenty of light."

"Were they wearing the same clothes?" Elizabeth asked, wiping up some ice cream that was trickling down her glass.

"Yes, they were," Amy replied.

To help her think, Elizabeth took another sip. "Well, their heads must have been covered," she said slowly, "so their mom couldn't see Clay's bald spot."

"Ray's," Amy corrected her.

"Whatever." Elizabeth grinned. "So were they wearing hats?"

"Yes," Amy admitted.

"And their left hands must have been covered, too, or else their mother would have seen the birthmark," Elizabeth added, carefully leaving out the names. She couldn't remember which twin was the one with the birthmark. "Were their left hands covered?"

Amy nodded reluctantly. "You're really close," she said.

"Were their right hands covered, too?" Elizabeth asked.

Now Amy looked triumphant. "No!" she said with a grin.

Left hands covered—but not right hands. Elizabeth frowned down into her soda. *When would you wear a glove on one hand but not on the other?* "Baseball!" she said suddenly, her eyes sparkling. "Of course!

They were baseball players. On their first day of practice, or something, so their mother didn't even have uniform numbers to help."

"Aw, you got it too easily," Amy said, sticking out her tongue at Elizabeth in mock anger.

"It's a tricky one," Elizabeth said sympathetically, lifting a spoonful of ice cream to her lips. She laughed to herself at the idea of Ray and Clay's mother, staring out at the field, not being able to tell which player was Ray and which was Clay. In their uniforms, hats, and mitts, they'd look exactly alike—

Wait a minute.

The spoon stopped halfway to Elizabeth's mouth. Her heart began to race double-time. *It's just like Joe,* she thought wildly. *All anyone has to go on is that clown costume! But it could have been anybody under that costume. It could have been Jeff, even!* Nervously Elizabeth licked her lips. *No one ever looks at a clown's real face—they only look at the makeup!*

"Are you all right?" Amy poked Elizabeth in the side.

"Umm—fine," Elizabeth answered. She took a big bite of the ice cream in front of her. "Just fine." *But how could Jeff get hold of the clown suit?* she wondered. *It's probably hanging in Joe's—* Then the answer struck her like a sudden bolt of lightning. *A key, of course! If Jeff had a key to Joe's apartment, then he could have "borrowed" the clown suit for a while—and no one would ever know.*

"E-liz-a-beth!" Amy waved her hand in front of her friend's face. "Are you in there?"

"Umm—yeah," Elizabeth answered, gently pushing Amy's arm back. "Listen, Amy, I have to—"

A crash cut her off.

"My soda!" Amy yelped.

Elizabeth blinked her eyes in dismay. Amy's elbow had knocked over the glass, and soda was pouring out at what seemed like a mile a minute.

"Oh, yuck," Amy said helplessly, watching the gooey mess spreading across the floor.

"I'll get a mop," Elizabeth promised, feeling terrible. *I know Amy knocked it over,* she said to herself, *but I was kind of pushing her arm back at the time—* Dashing behind the counter, she found Mr. Casey pushing buttons on a calculator in the back room. "We have a spill out there, Mr. Casey," she told him. "I'll take care of it—if you just tell me where to find a mop."

"Thanks." Mr. Casey's tired old eyes seemed to smile for a moment. He pointed to the brown door behind the telephone. "In there."

Elizabeth nodded and flung open the door. Inside was a small broom closet. Grabbing the mop and bucket, Elizabeth started to shut the door behind her. Then she stopped.

"Elizabeth!" Amy called. "It's getting all over the place!"

Elizabeth found her voice. "Just a minute!" Her eyes widened. In front of her was a piece of pegboard.

Hanging from the pegboard was a set of hooks.

Hanging from the hooks were keys.

Well, what do you know, Elizabeth told herself, eyes darting from one key to the next. *There's one marked* STOREROOM, *one marked* MARTIN CASEY—HOUSE, *and*—

And one silver key clearly labeled JOE—APARTMENT!

Eight

◇

Elizabeth hesitated for three seconds. Then her hand shot forward. Grabbing the silver key off its hook, she thrust it into the pocket of her shorts.

"Elizabeth!" Amy sounded in agony.

"Coming!" Elizabeth promised. Quickly, she hauled the bucket and the mop into the main room. The mess on the floor did look disgusting, all right. Elizabeth shoved the mop into the bucket.

"Elizabeth!" Amy hopped up and down on one foot. "You have to put water in the bucket!"

"Oops." Elizabeth stared at the mop. How had she forgotten that part? Patting the key to make sure it was still in her pocket, she turned on the faucet.

All I need now is Joe's address, she told herself nervously as she waited for the bucket to fill. *I could look it up in the phone book, or—*

"Mr. Casey?"

Sticking her head around the corner, Elizabeth gave old Mr. Casey what she hoped was her most dazzling smile. "Where does Joe live, exactly?"

"Seventy-three Holly Street," Mr. Casey mumbled absently, eyes scarcely lifting from the calculator.

"Thanks a lot," Elizabeth said quickly, measuring the distance in her mind. *Four blocks—no, three. Perfect! I'll sneak in and look for clues, maybe some signs that Joe might have been there, and then—*

"Elizabeth!" Amy wailed.

With a start Elizabeth looked back to the bucket. Water was overflowing onto the floor. "Oops." She giggled nervously. "I don't know why I'm such a space cadet today."

I feel bad about getting rid of Amy, Elizabeth thought a few minutes later as she walked quietly down the hallway in Joe's apartment building. *But spies have to be very secretive. I couldn't very well take her with me!*

Elizabeth paused outside the door to Joe's apartment, her heart hammering. Lifting the key to the lock, she wondered what would happen if she saw someone in the deserted hallway. *Just say you're Joe's cousin, picking up the mail,* she instructed herself. *No big deal.*

She fumbled with the key. *Of course, if I were really picking up the mail, I'd pick it up from the mailbox downstairs.*

Tensing every muscle in her body, Elizabeth thrust the key into the lock and turned it quickly. There was a click. Elizabeth closed her eyes in alarm, half expecting sirens to blast through her ears from every direction. But everything was quiet. After a moment, Elizabeth opened her eyes again. She was completely alone.

Here goes nothing. Elizabeth gave the door a gentle push. Slowly it swung open. Quickly she walked in, took the key out of the lock, and closed the door firmly behind her. She let out a sigh of relief, realizing that she'd been holding her breath.

Now what?

There wasn't much in the apartment. Elizabeth took a few steps forward and looked around. In one corner sat an old desk and chair that had obviously seen better days. In another corner, she could see a pullout bed. Most of the rest of the furniture was made from cardboard boxes and milk crates. Elizabeth shook her head. *Why did he give up that scholarship?*

Bending over, Elizabeth looked at the pile of papers on the desk. With trembling hands, she thumbed through the stack—a notice from the electric company, a bill for rent marked PAST DUE, a letter from a store. PLEASE REMIT AT ONCE was stamped in big red letters on the top of the phone bill. *Money trouble,* Elizabeth said to herself. *Ugh.*

To the left, the apartment led into a kitchen with a small refrigerator. Elizabeth opened it, feeling a little guilty. It contained nothing but two jars of peanut butter, a loaf of bread, and a container of milk. Elizabeth noticed that the expiration date on the milk was the day before yesterday. A carefully wrapped package was wedged into the freezer compartment. *Meat, maybe?* Elizabeth scratched her head and sighed. *How can anybody live on—just—this?*

Next to the kitchen was a small bathroom. Cautiously Elizabeth went in. A red rubber clown nose sat on top of the sink. A blue case was nearby. Opening it, Elizabeth shivered. *Clown makeup.* She couldn't help but see the robber in her mind's eye—

Enough of that, Elizabeth ordered herself, replacing the cover on the case. A lump of dread was forming in her stomach. All the clues seemed to point directly to Joe—the clown makeup, the unpaid bills. Nothing gave her any reason to suspect that Jeff might have been there. Crossing back into the main room, she noticed a walk-in closet near the door.

But before she could investigate it, she heard a sound in the hall.

Elizabeth turned and gasped. It was the sound of a key sliding into the lock!

There wasn't any choice. Grabbing the handle to the walk-in closet, Elizabeth dived inside and yanked the door shut behind her. Her heart pounded. Who in the world could be trying to open up the door? *I can't be caught,* she told herself firmly, clamping her lips tightly together. *I can't be!*

"That's funny," Elizabeth could hear a man say, "I could have sworn I'd locked that door."

"Well, maybe you didn't," a woman replied.

Elizabeth strained to catch the faintest glimmer of light in the closet, wondering how many people were out there.

The man spoke again. "This is crazy. I had the key in my hand—" He paused and laughed gently. "I can't stay on the force if I lose my mind like this all the time!"

Force, Elizabeth repeated to herself. *They must be police officers.* She was glad they weren't criminals, but she couldn't help worrying. After all, she figured, she was probably breaking the law by being there, even if she did have a key. Her heart thudded as she listened to the police officers moving around in the living room.

"Grab Carrey's bills," the policewoman instructed. "They need them as evidence for the trial."

"Right," the policeman responded. "Only—" He coughed. "Didn't you hear a noise a second ago?"

"What kind of a noise?" the woman asked.

"Search me." Ear to the door, Elizabeth thought she could hear footsteps coming her way. "Like a person scurrying around. You know. Maybe a door slamming?"

Elizabeth felt her whole body tense up.

"We could search the place, I guess," the policewoman suggested.

Oh, man, Elizabeth thought. Once again she realized

she was holding her breath. In the dim light, she could barely make out a row of what looked like long coats hanging behind her. *If I can only get back there,* she told herself.

Moving as quietly as she could, Elizabeth began to wiggle backward in the closet. *Don't open the door,* she begged the officers silently. *Please, please, don't open the door—*

"I guess we should." The man sighed. "I'll take the bathroom, you take the kitchen, OK?"

Good idea, Elizabeth thought. *And stay away from the closet!* She moved back, one tiny step at a time. Another step back—another—

What was that?

Elizabeth glanced down quickly, her heart beating furiously. She'd knocked her leg up against something cold and hard. Suppressing a scream, she peered at it more closely. *It won't hurt you,* she told herself sternly. *It's just made out of metal, that's all. It's only a—*

Elizabeth frowned. *A—foot.*

It can't possibly be a foot, she thought. *What would a metal foot be doing here in the closet?* Biting her lip, she stared at it again.

There was no doubt about it. *A foot and a lower leg—of a robot or something?* Had Joe ever talked to her about robots? She didn't think so.

But it has to be a robot foot, Elizabeth thought. *I mean, they don't make metal chickens nowadays—do they?*

She felt a rising sense of panic. *I don't want to*

stay in here any longer with this—this weird whatever-it-is! she thought, trying hard not to look at the metallic object in front of her.

Outside the closet, a door banged. "Nothing in here!" the policewoman announced.

Her partner sighed. "Nothing in the bathroom, either. Want to check under the bed?"

"Don't be silly, Lester," the woman snapped. "It's a pullout. No way anyone could hide underneath."

"All right." Elizabeth could almost hear Lester shrugging. "The closet, then?"

Here it comes, Elizabeth thought. She wriggled noiselessly into a tight ball and covered her head with her hands.

"Of course, I could have been hearing things . . . ," the policeman ventured.

Elizabeth felt as though she were going to burst. *Just decide,* she begged silently. *I can't stand the suspense anymore!*

The policewoman sighed loudly. "Yeah, you probably were. Grab the bills, Lester, and let's get out of here. And this time, don't forget to lock the door."

Ninety-eight . . . ninety-nine . . . one hundred, Elizabeth counted to herself. The police officers had left a few minutes before, and she'd counted to one hundred just to be safe.

Finally she stood up and crept to the closet door. She turned the handle, which creaked. Heart pounding, she let go and listened.

Nothing.

Bravely Elizabeth seized the handle again. This time she turned it slowly. She could feel the blood pulsing through her head as she flung the door open.

The closet flooded with light. Elizabeth blinked. But the room was empty.

Elizabeth let out her breath. Her whole body felt as if she'd gone for a ride in a washing machine. More than anything in the world, she wanted to get out of this apartment, to go back home where it was safe.

But there was one thing to do before she left. Turning slowly around, she stared at the metal thing in the closet. In the bright light of the room, she could see that it looked exactly as she'd thought. It *had* to be a robot leg. But where was the rest of the robot?

Well, that's a puzzle for another time, she thought, opening the door to Joe's apartment and walking into the empty hallway.

"*'Jay, I want to talk to you about your cousin.'*"

It was bedtime that night. Past bedtime, actually, Elizabeth noticed as she checked her clock. But she was almost done with her Amanda Howard mystery. In fact, there were only about ten pages to go. And Christine still hadn't been able to get Jay off the hook for murdering his aunt.

"Go, Christine!" Elizabeth muttered. Time was running short. Usually Christine had found the real killer by now.

"'You mean Chauncey?' Jay gave a hollow laugh. 'What about him?'"

"Christine looked Jay straight in the eye. 'I haven't been able to find one scrap of evidence against him.'

"Jay drew in his breath.

"'I'm sorry,' Christine continued hastily. 'I'll keep looking, of course. I've gotten you released from prison—for now, anyway. And I know in my heart that your cousin must be guilty. Even so . . .' She hesitated.

"Jay shook his head. 'Christine,' he said slowly, placing his hand on her arm, 'I'm counting on you.'"

Elizabeth looked up for a moment. She had to concentrate on breathing evenly. The book was making her almost as nervous as she had been in Joe's closet.

Ten minutes later, Elizabeth turned to the last page of the book. Her stomach was doing flip-flops inside her. *It can't be true!* she thought desperately.

But it was.

"The corners of Jay's mouth turned up in an evil-looking grin. 'You really fell for it, didn't you?' he asked sardonically.

"Christine's smile faded, but she held her ground. 'Perhaps I did,' she replied firmly. 'So you were the guilty one all along.'

"'You bet.' Jay seemed to spit out the words. 'I knew you'd believe any sob story I'd tell you. I also knew you'd find any evidence there was against my cousin.'

"'Thank you,' Christine murmured.

"'It's just too bad there wasn't any,' Jay went on. 'But I really had you hopping, didn't I? Ha!' Throwing his head back, he laughed long and loud.

"Christine set her jaw and motioned to the authorities who were concealed behind her. 'But it's I who will have the last laugh, Jay Carroll,' she said, tapping a small microphone attached to her body. 'Because you're going to jail!'

"A strange look came over Jay's face. He tried to speak, but he was restrained by an officer. 'Jay Carroll, I charge you with the murder of your aunt,' he declared.

"And Christine nodded her head sadly."

Elizabeth slammed the book shut. It was all she could do to keep from throwing it across the room. She snapped off the light and got under the covers. Usually she would have appreciated a surprise ending like this one. But not today.

In the darkness, Elizabeth licked her lips nervously. *What if Christine isn't the only one who makes mistakes?*

Nine

"So what's wrong with you, anyway?" Jessica asked the next morning. She took a bite of French toast and sat back to look at her sister. "You look terrible."

"Gee, thanks," Elizabeth murmured. She sliced off a tiny piece of toast and pushed it around her plate with her fork.

Jessica wrinkled her nose. "No offense, Lizzie," she continued, "but you look like you haven't slept in about a year." She was about to add that Elizabeth usually ate more than three bites of French toast, when the phone rang.

Jessica stood up quickly and ran to answer it.

"Hi, Jessica," Lila answered once Jessica picked up. "I'm over at the courthouse. The trial's about to start."

"The trial?" Jessica frowned.

"You know, Joe Carrey's trial?" Lila sounded exasperated. "The guy who robbed the pharmacy and knocked you down? It *was* you, wasn't it?"

"Oh," Jessica said wisely. "Joe." She glanced at her sister. Elizabeth's head snapped up and a pained expression came over her face.

"So anyway," Lila went on, "my dad knows this guy who works—"

For the sheriff's department, Jessica filled in silently.

"—for the sheriff's department," Lila continued, "and he says it's going to be a real short trial. Like, maybe, a day or two. And he says Joe's going to be found guilty."

"Uh-huh," Jessica said, casting another quick look at Elizabeth.

"And he thinks Joe *should* be found guilty, too," Lila said, unable to keep the satisfaction out of her voice. "He says all the evidence is very clear." She paused for breath. "Isn't it cool that we know a real live armed robber, Jess?"

Jessica stared straight ahead, but she could feel Elizabeth's eyes on her. "Umm, well—"

"And by the way, Jessica," Lila went on before Jessica could say any more, "your silly sister's not still on this Joe-is-innocent kick, is she?"

"Leave her out of this," Jessica snapped, suddenly feeling protective of her sister. Suddenly it was clear to her why Elizabeth looked so out of it. She was worried about Joe. "She can believe what she wants, OK?"

Lila sighed. "All right. Whatever you say, Jess. I just thought you might like to know what's going on. Well, gotta go." There was a click.

Slowly Jessica put down the phone.

"What was that all about, Jess?" Elizabeth asked. Her voice sounded weak and hurried.

Jessica managed a smile. "Oh, nothing. Nothing important." She walked back to the table. But an image had popped into her head, an image that wouldn't go away: Joe in a cramped prison cell, Joe locked up for years and years and years, Joe not coming out of prison until he was about eighty-five and had long flowing white hair.

Jessica bit her lip. She didn't like the picture at all. She stabbed a slice of French toast with her fork. On the other hand, if Joe were innocent, then the police would have to find the real criminal. And that might make people think some more about why she went down to the pharmacy that night. *Do I really want to draw attention to the maxipad business again?*

Jessica pushed away her plate. She suddenly wasn't hungry. And she had the feeling that no matter how the trial turned out, she wouldn't be too happy.

Elizabeth stared at the clock, willing the hands to move a little faster. She had never felt so incredibly bored. It was three thirty in the afternoon, and she was the only one at home. She'd been reading the same page in her social studies book for what felt like hours. Somehow she couldn't concentrate. She was too worried about Joe.

The phone rang, but Elizabeth didn't feel like answering it. After a few rings, the answering machine picked up. Lila's voice boomed out into the living room. "Hi, Jessica!" she said. "It's me, Lila. I'm calling from the courthouse again, and guess what? They found the gun." Lila's voice dropped down to a whisper. "And you'll never believe where it was."

Elizabeth tensed her muscles, wanting to hear and yet not wanting to hear at the same time.

"In Joe's apartment!" Lila exclaimed. "Isn't that just amazingly awesome!"

No, Elizabeth screamed to herself. She clutched her hands to her ears, wondering if she should go switch the machine off altogether. But Lila was speaking again. "It was in the freezer compartment of Joe's refrigerator! All wrapped up like a bundle of meat! What a hiding place, huh?" Lila laughed merrily. "They found it this morning when they went back and searched the place again. Well, talk to you later!" Lila hung up.

In the freezer compartment. Elizabeth sat completely still. She could scarcely believe it. *That package I saw yesterday—that must have been the gun!*

A few moments before, Elizabeth had thought she couldn't feel any worse—but now she knew she was wrong. There was just too much evidence now. The clown suit, the gun, Joe's need for money.

All the clues pointed toward one horrible fact: Joe Carrey, armed robber. Guilty as charged.

Well here goes, Elizabeth thought, stepping into Casey's later that afternoon. She wasn't really in the mood for ice cream, but she knew she had to return Joe's key. *Not that he'll be needing it anytime soon.*

Mr. Casey was busy scrubbing up a spill down at one end of the counter, and Jeff was waiting on a table near the window. Elizabeth crept behind the counter and into the broom closet.

Quickly she replaced the key on the proper hook. *Thank goodness that's done,* she told herself. But as she turned to leave, a shadow fell over her. Elizabeth jerked her head upward. Jeff was blocking her path.

"What do you think you're doing?" he demanded, brandishing a broom.

"Umm—umm—" Elizabeth's mind whirled. "I was just—"

"You didn't go into the broom closet, did you?" Jeff pressed. He took a step closer and stared menacingly at Elizabeth.

"Umm—I mean," Elizabeth said desperately. *Why is he so concerned about the broom closet?* "That is—"

"Calm down, Jeff." Mr. Casey looked over from the counter. "The poor kid's probably looking for the bathroom, that's all."

"That's right," Elizabeth said quickly. "The bathroom. I, umm, uh, forgot where it was."

Jeff jerked his thumb in the direction of the bathrooms. "Over there," he growled. "You're in here enough, you and your friends. You ought to know that."

"Umm—yeah," Elizabeth said, nodding. "I should, but, well . . ." She cleared her throat. "Sometimes I kind of get my right and my left mixed up. Sorry," she added humbly.

Jeff laid down his broom. "If you've got to go, then *go*," he snapped, his eyes glittering.

Elizabeth pushed past him and headed for the bathrooms in the corner of the store. Turning around just before she reached the door, she gulped. Mr. Casey had gone back to his work, but Jeff was standing in front of the broom closet as if he were a barricade. He was staring directly at her, and a deep frown was creasing his face.

"I'll be watching you from now on," he said in a soft but menacing voice.

"Did you hear Lila's message, Lizzie?" Jessica asked soon after Elizabeth arrived home.

Elizabeth nodded gloomily. "I heard it," she muttered, sitting down on the hallway steps.

Jessica sat down next to her. "Then you know—"

"Yup." Elizabeth turned away.

"Hey, I have something to tell you!" Jessica put her hand on her twin's shoulder. It was all Elizabeth could do not to shake it off. "It's this great new brainteaser. This woman—"

Elizabeth groaned. A new brainteaser? The last thing she wanted to use was her brain. Right now she couldn't focus on anything besides guns in freezers and robot legs in closets and clown makeup and unpaid stacks of bills. "I'm sorry, Jess," she said, trying not to look her sister in the eye. "Some other time, OK? I'm really tired."

"Oh, come on," Jessica pleaded. "It'll help take your mind off things."

"No, really," Elizabeth insisted, standing and heading upstairs.

"But this one's so *good*," Jessica insisted, hustling ahead and blocking Elizabeth's path. "I'll make it quick. Please?"

Elizabeth sighed. There didn't seem to be any way out of it. "All right. Just make it quick."

"Sure," Jessica agreed. "Awomangoestosleepand—"

"Not *that* quick." Elizabeth couldn't help smiling.

Jessica rolled her eyes. "All right. A woman goes to sleep. When she wakes up, she's lost something."

"Too bad," Elizabeth commented.

"*Not* too bad." Jessica's voice held a note of triumph. "She's a whole lot happier than when she went to sleep. What did she lose?"

Elizabeth frowned. "All right," she said, growing interested despite herself. "Did the woman fall asleep in her own bed?"

Jessica shook her head, grinning.

Elizabeth raised an eyebrow. "OK, was it in a bed at all?"

"Nope," Jessica answered smugly.

Elizabeth leaned against the wall. "Did she lose something small? Like, smaller than my hand?"

"*Very* small," Jessica agreed importantly.

"Something you could see?" Elizabeth pressed.

"Oh yeah, you could see it," Jessica replied. Her eyes twinkled. "But maybe we should finish this up later. I mean, I've taken up enough of your time. If you've got other things to do—"

Elizabeth grabbed her sister's arm. "Those things can wait," she said urgently. She had to admit, Jessica was right. Thinking about something besides Joe *did* make her feel better. And at that moment all she really wanted to do was solve the brainteaser.

"Pretty cute," Elizabeth said slowly. It had taken her about fifteen minutes to solve the puzzle, and she was feeling proud of herself. "The woman had a terrible toothache, and she was put to sleep in a dentist's chair. Then they pulled the tooth—so she lost it."

"That's right." Jessica nodded.

"And of course she was much happier after they'd taken it out." Elizabeth grinned. "I like that one."

"I knew you would," Jessica said, patting her twin on the back. "Now you can go do what you wanted to do before."

"Right. Thanks, Jess."

That brainteaser was really cool, Elizabeth thought

as she mounted the stairs and entered her bedroom.
*She loses a tooth. Of course, a tooth. I kept thinking it
was money or a jewel or something like that, but it turned
out to be a part of her own body!* Shaking her head, she
walked into her room. *A part of her own body—*

Wait a minute.

Elizabeth stood very still. An idea had just oc-
curred to her.

"P-r-o—p-r-o- . . ." Her heart beating rapidly,
Elizabeth flipped through her father's medical en-
cyclopedia. "'Pneumonia,' 'psoriasis' . . ."

Running her finger along the page, she located
the word she was looking for. "'Prosthesis,'" she
said aloud, feeling the word slide off her tongue.
"'An artificial substitute for a missing body part.'"
Elizabeth's pulse quickened. "'Especially, an artificial arm or leg.'" *Or leg,* she repeated silently.

Next to the words, there was a picture of an object that looked awfully familiar. "*A typical pros-
thetic leg,*" the text began. "*Made with high-tech
metal, the 'foot' bears weight and allows the wearer
many possible activities, though of course it does not
transmit sensations of pain . . .*"

No pain, Elizabeth thought, remembering how
Joe had barely noticed when she'd stepped so hard
on his foot a few days earlier.

She squinted at the picture again. *No doubt about
it. That's what I saw in Joe's closet!*

Suddenly it all became clear. Joe was missing a

leg! *That's why he always wears long pants, no matter how hot it is outside. That's why he doesn't ride a motorcycle anymore. That's why he quit the track team and gave up his scholarship.*

Elizabeth slammed the book shut.

But how can I prove it?

Ten

"Lost his leg, huh?" Wendy frowned. It was later that afternoon. Elizabeth had biked over to the college library as fast as she could—there had been no time to wait for a bus. "It makes a lot of sense, now that I think about it."

Elizabeth nodded vigorously. "That's what I thought, too," she said, the words running over each other in her excitement. "I was thinking maybe there was an accident, and I could look it up in the newspaper, or something. You *do* have Sweet Valley newspapers here, don't you?" she asked hopefully.

Wendy bit her lip. "We do, but it would be awful to check." She waved her hand toward a room behind her. "The papers are all in there, on microfilm. You need to use a special machine to read them, and I'll show you how if you like. But there's no index, and you don't know when the accident happened, if it ever did. You'd have to begin at the beginning of that summer and—" She shook her head. "It would take you forever."

Elizabeth's heart sank. "But—"

"Microfilm hurts most people's eyes, too," Wendy continued. "And even if there was an accident, it might not have made the papers."

"But—" Elizabeth tried again, determination in her voice. She couldn't quit now. "I don't care how long it takes," she said. "I'm going to try to find it!"

Elizabeth sighed and loaded the third reel of microfilm onto the machine. Wendy had been right, she admitted sadly. She was getting nowhere fast.

The microfilm was hard to read, just as Wendy had said, and Elizabeth's eyes were getting tired of squinting at the print. She'd realized early on that she didn't have to read all the articles, just the headlines, but there had hardly been any accidents at all in Sweet Valley that summer, it seemed. At least, hardly any that made the papers. And none involving a college student named Joe Carrey.

"Any luck yet?" Wendy collected the other two reels of film and put them back in their boxes.

"No," Elizabeth admitted gloomily, threading the tape carefully through the viewer. "And I'm only up to early July."

"Bummer," Wendy said. She looked thoughtful.

"You know . . ." Her voice trailed off. "Seems to me there was some kind of awful accident that month involving a couple of trucks and a motorcycle."

A motorcycle? Elizabeth snapped her head up.

"I don't remember any of the details," Wendy went on, "but it was just before my birthday. That's the twenty-second. Maybe that'll give you a clue."

"Worth a try," Elizabeth said, pushing the fast-forward button. "Thanks!"

Oh, man, Elizabeth thought uneasily, staring at the screen in front of her. *Oh, man.*

The headline appeared on the middle of page three in the July 21 newspaper. *Four hurt in fiery crash,* Elizabeth read, her eyes flicking nervously toward the photo next to the story. *A truck with a smashed front end—a streetlight knocked over—*

And the twisted remains of a motorcycle. Oh, man.

"That's his bike." Wendy peered over Elizabeth's shoulder. She sounded distracted. "Sheesh. I never knew."

"'A terrible crash took place yesterday morning on State Highway 1121,'" Elizabeth read aloud. "Sounds like one of the trucks turned too suddenly and never even saw the motorcycle." She drew in her breath. *Not "the" motorcycle. Joe's motorcycle.*

"Here you go." Wendy tapped the bottom of the page. "'The motorcyclist was taken to the hospital, his left leg badly mangled below the knee. He has been identified as'"—her finger slowly traced the line—"'Sweet Valley University student Joseph Carrey.'"

"I guess that clinches it," Elizabeth said. Her mouth felt dry. "How terribly, terribly sad."

"He never breathed a word about it, either." Wendy pulled her lips into a tight line. "I wonder why."

"He hid it awfully well," Elizabeth agreed.

Wendy shook her head. "He must have spent hours making sure nobody knew." She raised her hands and let them drop. "People here would have been supportive, I know they would!"

Elizabeth felt a sudden flare of anger at Joe, for not confiding in people, for making her go through all these newspapers, for hiding his injury. She shook her head. Besides, having a terrible accident didn't make him innocent of the robbery.

Did it?

"More sports highlights?" Elizabeth asked Steven, who was sprawled out in the family room, a big bowl of popcorn in his lap. It was ten o'clock at night, but she was feeling too restless—and too confused and upset about Joe—to get ready for bed.

"Yup," Steven said happily. "Got to find out how all the baseball games came out. Hey, look at this play."

Elizabeth watched as an outfielder picked up the ball and threw it toward home plate. The catcher caught it and stabbed at a runner who was sliding in.

"He's going to be safe!" Steven exclaimed. "Great slide, huh?"

"I thought he looked out," Elizabeth said, watching the umpire signal safe, just as Steven had predicted.

"We'll show you the throw from a different angle," the sportscaster declared.

Elizabeth saw another camera picking up the same action. This time it was clear that the runner had gotten there first. "How could you tell?" she asked Steven curiously.

Steven grinned sheepishly. "These are just highlights. I saw the game live this afternoon," he admitted.

Elizabeth laughed and watched as the highlight video showed the play three more times, switching between the two angles.

"Well, I'm going to bed," Elizabeth decided finally. "Don't stay up too late."

"No problem," Steven said, his mouth full of popcorn.

Elizabeth went back upstairs and got into bed. The image of the baseball player sliding into home stayed in her head as she turned off the light. She closed her eyes, trying hard not to think about Joe and the trial, and waited for sleep.

But something wouldn't let her.

In her mind's eye she saw strange pictures

flashing over and over. *Just like Steven's sports show,* she thought drowsily. There she was stepping on the artificial leg in Joe's dark closet—and then she was stepping on Joe's foot at Casey's.

And then the picture changed again, to the clown in the pharmacy, hopping up and down on one foot and yelling after Jessica had kicked him—and then, exactly like Steven's highlight video, the pictures all played themselves over again. The artificial leg . . . and stepping on Joe's foot . . . and the clown yelling in the pharmacy . . .

Until Elizabeth finally dropped off to sleep.

Eleven

◇

"Steven, how do you like your pancakes?" Jessica asked the next morning. She had woken up feeling inspired to make breakfast for her family.

"Not burned," Steven said from behind a mouthful of cereal. "Not like last time."

"What was the problem with last time?" Jessica snapped.

"You mean when you practically burned the house down?" Steven snorted.

Jessica searched her mind for an appropriate response, but before she could say anything Elizabeth rushed into the kitchen wearing a nightgown, a wild look on her face. "He didn't do it!" she gasped.

"Huh?" Jessica wrinkled her nose.

"Joe! Joe didn't do it! I mean, he didn't commit

the robbery!" Elizabeth grabbed Jessica by the shoulders.

"Hey, lay off!" Jessica said, trying to flip a pancake. "What are you talking about, anyway?"

"Joe couldn't have done it!" By now Jessica felt like she was being shaken to pieces. "He's missing his left leg below the knee and—"

"He's *what*?" Jessica turned to stare at her sister. "Are you out of your mind or something?"

"Yes, how on earth would you know a thing like that?" Mr. Wakefield put in, buttering a piece of toast.

Elizabeth waved her hand dismissively. "I'll explain later. Anyway, Jess, when you ran into the clown that night—"

"I did not 'run into' the clown that night," Jessica informed her. "We had a *collision*."

"Whatever." Elizabeth rolled her eyes. "You kicked him in the left shin. The *left* shin, right? I mean, correct?"

Jessica frowned. She couldn't see what difference it could possibly make, but she thought back to the scene in the pharmacy. *The clown, standing there, holding one foot in the air and yelling bloody blue murder. And that foot had a shoe—a shoe marked—* "You're right," she admitted. "He got kicked just above the shoe marked L. On the left shin."

"And Joe doesn't *have* a left shin!" Elizabeth burst out triumphantly. "So he couldn't have been the robber! Don't you *see*?"

Jessica looked at her sister skeptically. "OK.

Assuming for a minute that Joe doesn't have a left leg, well, I guess you're right. He couldn't have been the robber." She waved the spatula in the air. "But what exactly makes you think Joe doesn't have a left leg?"

Elizabeth turned slightly pink. Before she could say anything, though, Steven broke in. "Do I smell something burning?" he demanded. "Like a pancake?"

"Oh, no," Jessica lied, looking down in a panic. *Oh, yuck.* Using the spatula, she quickly scraped the blackened mess into the garbage can. "Nothing like a pancake at all!"

"So someone told you that Joe had an artificial leg?" Mr. Wakefield looked puzzled.

Elizabeth gulped. She was now sitting at the kitchen table. "Umm—yeah," she said, trying not to catch her father's eye. She didn't want to mention having broken into Joe's apartment.

"And you don't remember who this 'someone' is." Mr. Wakefield frowned.

"Umm . . ." Elizabeth licked her lips. "Not exactly."

"Very common," Steven muttered. He finished his cereal and went back for another helping, since the pancakes still hadn't arrived. "When bad things happen to people—like being in a robbery—sometimes they can't even remember their own names. It's called post-traumatic stress disorder," he added importantly. "We learned about it in school when we were studying the Vietnam War."

"Right." Elizabeth decided to shift to a safer topic. "Anyway, then I went to look it up in the newspaper. And he was in an accident, that's for sure."

Mrs. Wakefield's eyes widened. "And he lost his leg? It said that?"

"Well, not quite," Elizabeth admitted. "It said his leg was badly mangled. I looked in the paper for the next few days, too, and it didn't say anything about the leg being amputated. They didn't mention him again, actually."

"Badly mangled," Mr. Wakefield repeated, tapping his chin thoughtfully. "Well, I suppose it's possible . . ."

"Yes!" Elizabeth broke in. "Don't you *see*? It all makes so much sense!"

"It does." Mr. Wakefield looked at his wife and then back at Elizabeth. "All right, Elizabeth. I have a feeling there's something you're not telling us, but I'll let it go for now. The question is—" He looked at Mrs. Wakefield once more.

"Can we save an innocent man?" Mrs. Wakefield finished.

A rush of adrenaline shot through Elizabeth. She grabbed for her mother's hand. "I *know* we can. All we have to do is get Jessica to testify in court— today!" She beamed at her sister.

Jessica turned from the stove abruptly. She was slightly pale. "All we have to do is *what*?"

*   *   *

Maybe I just imagined what Jess was saying, Elizabeth told herself a few minutes later. She'd gone up to her room to get dressed. *I mean, she seemed upset, but she was kind of vague about it. She'll probably be psyched to help. She likes Joe, too. Almost as much as I do.*

Elizabeth grabbed a clean T-shirt from her drawer. *Yup, I must have imagined it,* she thought.

There was a knock on the door. "Come in!" Elizabeth called out, pulling the shirt over her head.

Jessica entered the room, a deep frown etched across her face. "I want you to know that there is *no possible way* I will testify at Joe's trial," she said. "You can get that idea out of your mind right this minute!"

Elizabeth felt a wave of dread slowly washing over her. "But—but why not?"

"Because." Jessica thrust her chin forward belligerently. "You want me to tell the whole world that I acted like a klutz?" she demanded. "You want me to tell everybody that I was buying you-know-whats like a total doofus, like a banana brain?"

"But, Jess!" Elizabeth interrupted. "Everybody buys maxipads. And you didn't act like a klutz when you—"

"You said so yourself." Jessica balled her fingers into fists. "You said, 'when you *ran into* the clown.' Those were your exact words!"

"But—" Elizabeth felt as though the bottom was

dropping out of her world. *How can Jessica act this way?* She gave a nervous little laugh. "You don't really mean it, do you? Why don't you, umm . . ." Elizabeth thought hard. "Umm, you know, go take a nap or something, then maybe you'll feel better."

"Yeah, right." Jessica didn't move.

"Why didn't you tell me before?" Elizabeth asked desperately. "You didn't mention any of this downstairs."

"In front of Steven?" Jessica gave a hollow laugh. "Talk about *maxipads* in front of my *brother*? And your brother, too, I might add? Give me a break." She shook her head. "He'd tease me for the rest of my life—and so would everybody else."

"But—" Elizabeth tried to get a word in edgewise. "You don't have to say what you were buying, you know. You can just—"

"They'll show the video," Jessica said flatly. "*Lila* is watching the trial. I bet some other *friends* of ours are watching the trial. I am *not* about to let them see me waving that box of pads around like a dork." She took a step forward. "There might even be someone we know on the jury. Do you understand?"

Elizabeth looked at her sister pleadingly. "You can't let that stop you," she argued. "Joe needs—"

"Then *you* do it." Jessica spat out the words.

"But—but—" *You were the one who kicked the clown,* Elizabeth thought frantically. *You're the only one who could feel that there was a real leg under that outfit.* "An innocent man's life may be at stake!"

she said at last. "How can you say no?"

"Like this," Jessica said. She leaned close to Elizabeth's face and formed her mouth into a perfect circle. *"No!"*

Elizabeth sat in stunned silence. Across the hall, she could hear Jessica's door slamming shut. A moment later, there was a faint click. *She's locked herself in,* she told herself bitterly. *Jessica, how can you do this to me? To Joe?*

Her mind whirled. *Can't we somehow force her to testify? What if I tell Mom and Dad? What if I tell Joe's lawyers?*

Elizabeth got up from the bed and began to pace. "There's something in the Constitution," she said slowly. "The right to a fair trial. Yes. Jessica can't break the Constitution, can she?" For a moment Elizabeth felt hopeful. Then she grimaced. Deep down, she knew the truth. No army in the world could get her sister to do anything she didn't want to.

If we made her get on the witness stand, she'd probably deny the whole thing, she said to herself. *She'd say, "Who?"* Elizabeth rolled her eyes, the way Jessica would. *She'd say, "That girl on the screen? You mean the one in the pink sweater? I never saw her before in my life!"* She shook her head sorrowfully. *And because she's so stubborn, Joe will probably go to jail. For—for years.*

Elizabeth crossed the room to her sweater

drawer and pulled out the pink one on top. Unexpectedly she felt a lump in her throat. *Pink,* she thought. *Just like—*

Elizabeth narrowed her eyes as she stared at the pink sweater in her hand. The pink sweater with the EW monogram across the chest. The sweater Jessica had worn to the pharmacy that night.

Elizabeth glanced up at her reflection in the mirror, and suddenly she had an idea. An idea too incredible to ignore.

Twelve

"I still can't figure it out, Elizabeth," Mrs. Wakefield mused, settling into the passenger seat of the family van later that morning. The Wakefields were heading to the courtroom, where Elizabeth was to be a surprise witness in the trial.

"Figure out what?" Elizabeth asked.

"The way your memory works, I guess." Mrs. Wakefield closed the van door after her. "I don't understand how you could forget it was you who kicked the clown, not Jessica."

"Oh, that." Elizabeth felt her face flush. *I know it sounds a little weird*, she thought, *but what choice do I have?* "Don't you remember, Mom?" she said as brightly as she could. "Even when I said it at breakfast, Jessica knew I was wrong right away. Remember? Jess said, 'I did not run into the clown.'"

Mr. Wakefield started the engine. "Still seems weird to me. When I talked to Joe's lawyer this morning, she said of course she'd use you in the trial, but—"

"I keep telling you, it's post-traumatic stress disorder, Dad," Steven piped up. He was sitting in the backseat with Elizabeth. "That's probably why Jessica locked herself in her room and won't come out—post-traumatic stress disorder."

"Hmm." Mrs. Wakefield didn't sound convinced. "I guess what's really hard for me to understand is what you *did* remember."

"Huh?" Elizabeth bit her lip.

"Well, I just think it's strange that you know which of the clown's two feet you kicked," Mrs. Wakefield went on, "but you couldn't even remember if it was you or Jessica. To hang on to a little detail like that . . ." Her voice trailed off.

"Oh, *that*," Elizabeth said dismissively. "It's just that Jess and I sometimes have a little confusion about which of us is which. You know, being twins and all."

Mrs. Wakefield glanced at her daughter. "Funny, I don't seem to remember your mentioning this before . . ."

"Mom!" Steven sounded irritated. "It's just post-traumatic stress disorder, is all! Why won't you listen to me? Happens a *lot*. Especially when people think they might be about to have to testify."

Yup, Elizabeth thought, managing a weak smile.

Her stomach was doing flip-flops. *I don't know if it's post-traumatic stressful whatever or not, but people who are about to testify definitely don't feel so great.*

The courtroom was a large and forbidding place. Elizabeth looked nervously around. Next to her sat a man in black robes. *The judge,* Elizabeth told herself. To her right were twelve men and women. *The jury.*

Elizabeth stared directly into the audience. Lila and Mandy were there, along with a lot of people she didn't know. Probably reporters, she figured. Jeff sat near the back. Elizabeth wondered why in the world he was there. Next to him was old Mr. Casey, looking older and more miserable than ever.

Elizabeth swung all the way around. To her left sat a very familiar figure. Joe.

Elizabeth tried hard to give him an inspiring smile, but she couldn't quite manage one. *I don't think I've ever been so nervous before,* she thought, realizing that her knees were shaking. *I just hope I make it!*

Joe's lawyer, a short, dark-haired woman named Ms. Simmons, stood and gave Elizabeth a reassuring smile. "Your Honor, here is the witness I mentioned this morning."

"Miss Wakefield," the judge said gravely. "We're glad you're here. Are you ready to be sworn in?"

Sworn in? Elizabeth vaguely remembered having seen movies in which witnesses were sworn in. But she couldn't remember any of the details. "I—I guess so," she heard someone say in an unusually high-pitched voice. It took a moment before she realized the voice was her own. She swallowed hard. "I mean, yes. Yes, sir."

The judge nodded. The court clerk stood up. "Raiseyourrighthand," he said, running his words together, "andrepeatafterme."

Of course! Elizabeth thought, raising her right hand. *This is when I promise to tell the truth and nothing but the truth.*

She took a deep breath. Her stomach hurt.

I'll do the best I can!

"Miss Wakefield," Ms. Simmons said, "please describe for the court the clothing worn by the robber."

"Sure." Elizabeth nodded. Things had been going pretty smoothly since the questioning had begun. She was almost enjoying being on the witness stand. *Of course,* she thought, *the hard part is still to come.* "He had on a pair of oversize brown shoes, a fright wig—" She screwed up her face to remember.

"Take your time." The judge's voice was quiet but firm.

"And—umm—a red-and-blue clown suit, with a big yellow button, and a, you know, a fringy thing on his chest." Unable to think of a better word, Elizabeth stroked the front of her shirt.

A thin man dressed in a suit stood up at the table next to Joe's. "Your Honor," he demanded, "what is the point of this exercise?" *The prosecutor,* Elizabeth reminded herself, *the one who's trying to prove that Joe's guilty.* "The store clerk described all this before, and I hardly see—"

"Give us a minute," Ms. Simmons interrupted. She turned to the judge. "Everything will become clear."

Elizabeth stared from the prosecutor to Ms. Simmons and back. "Please continue, Ms. Simmons," the judge said at last. Eyes flashing angrily, the prosecutor sat back down.

"Thank you." Ms. Simmons faced Elizabeth again. "Now, Miss Wakefield, we're going to show you the video of the robbery, and we'd like you to talk us through it, all right?"

Elizabeth took a deep breath and nodded.

A moment later, a television was brought into the courtroom and the familiar videotape began to play. Ms. Simmons looked at Elizabeth expectantly.

"OK," Elizabeth began slowly, nibbling at her fingernail. "That's, umm, me and my sister waiting in line to buy, umm—" She hesitated. "To buy that box."

Ms. Simmons nodded. "That's you holding the—umm—box of sanitary napkins, am I right?"

Elizabeth bit her lip. She pointed to the image of her sister, who was clutching the maxipads box. "You can see my initials on the shirt," she said, trying to sound as calm as possible. *And it's the truth, too,* she reminded herself. *You* can *see my initials on the shirt!*

On the screen, Elizabeth saw Jessica back up and kick the robber swiftly in the shin.

"And how did the robber react when you kicked him?" Ms. Simmons went on.

Elizabeth felt her heart skip a beat, remembering that she was under oath to tell the truth. "The robber started jumping up and down when he was kicked," she said at last, pleased with how she'd phrased her answer. "And you can't see it on the screen, but he was yelling loudly, too."

"In other words, he seemed badly hurt." Ms. Simmons moved a step closer to Elizabeth.

Elizabeth took a quick look at Joe. He was sitting up a little straighter, she realized, and there was a thoughtful look in his eyes. "He acted hurt," she said truthfully.

The prosecutor made an impatient noise. "Your Honor—"

"Which shin was injured when the robber was kicked, Miss Wakefield?" Ms. Simmons went on, calmly ignoring the prosecutor.

That was an easy one. "The left," Elizabeth said firmly.

Joe's lawyer pressed a button on the VCR. "The court will please note that the robber was kicked in the left shin," she said briskly, replaying the tape.

"So noted," the judge said with a sigh. "Please, Ms. Simmons, you are trying the patience—"

"The left shin," Ms. Simmons continued quickly, looking straight at Elizabeth. "Now, Miss

Wakefield, could you identify the man who robbed the pharmacy? Do you see him in the court?"

There was a sudden hush.

Elizabeth's eyes flickered around the audience. It seemed that everyone was waiting eagerly for her answer. *Lila and Mandy, Steven, Jeff—*

"Is he here in the courtroom?" Ms. Simmons repeated.

Elizabeth could see a contemptuous look on Jeff's face. *I bet he is,* she said under her breath. *I just bet he is!*

But of course she had no evidence to back it up.

"I don't know," she said aloud, her words echoing in the stillness. "But I know who it isn't."

No one said a word. Elizabeth saw Joe lean a little farther forward, his face a mixture of curiosity and fear. Somewhere in the audience, a piece of paper rustled.

Ms. Simmons bent down and stared directly into Elizabeth's face. "Who can't it be?"

"It can't be the defendant, Joe Carrey," Elizabeth said, her voice gathering in weight and volume as she spoke.

"And why can't it be Joe Carrey, Miss Wakefield?" Ms. Simmons pressed.

Elizabeth licked her lips and focused her gaze on Joe's face. "Because Joe doesn't have a left shin."

The room exploded into conversation. "Objection!" the prosecutor called out, standing up so quickly, he nearly lost his balance. Elizabeth saw

Lila talking excitedly to Mandy. Jeff was on his feet nearby, yelling to the prosecutor, an angry expression on his face. Two reporters scratched away on their pads. Mrs. Wakefield nervously twisted the sleeve of her dress. *Well, I did it*, Elizabeth thought, catching her breath. Above the hubbub she heard the judge pounding his gavel.

Then she turned to Joe.

Joe sat stock-still, his blue eyes looking haunted. *I'm sorry, Joe*, she told him silently, almost wishing she could take back what she'd said. *But it's for your own good, really it is!*

"Order!" The judge's voice boomed through the courtroom. Gradually the clamor died down. "Objection overruled," the judge went on, turning to the prosecutor. "Mr. Carrey, the court has a request. Would you please approach the bench and roll up your left pant leg to the knee?"

Elizabeth bit her lip.

For a moment, Joe didn't move. Then a small smile began to creep over his face.

"Mr. Carrey." The judge sounded disapproving.

"Yes, Your Honor." With a sudden movement, Joe stood up and walked firmly toward the judge.

Elizabeth held her breath and leaned forward. Slowly, Joe bent down. The courtroom was absolutely quiet as he grasped the cuff of his left pant leg and began to roll it up.

Elizabeth could hardly stand the suspense, but at the same time, she was almost afraid to find out the truth. Finally Joe stood in front of her, his pant leg rolled up to the knee.

And a metal prosthesis was clearly visible underneath it.

The prosecutor began to shout. Three jury members turned to one another and launched into conversation. Elizabeth could see Mandy getting to her feet, clapping and cheering. Somewhere in the audience, flashbulbs popped. Over the noise, Elizabeth could hear Ms. Simmons's voice. "The defense rests its case!"

He showed us his secret, Elizabeth thought happily, blinking back tears. She stared at Joe, who was looking with wide eyes at his lawyer. *He did it!*

"Has the jury reached a verdict?"

Elizabeth watched nervously as the twelve members of the jury settled themselves back into their seats. They'd been discussing the case in private for less than an hour. She only hoped they had good news.

The head juror nodded and passed a sheet of paper to the clerk. "We have, Your Honor."

The clerk began to read. " 'Wethejury—' "

"A little slower, please," the judge interrupted.

The clerk shrugged. " 'We the jury,' " he read, pausing carefully after each word, " 'find the defendant . . .' "

He paused.

" 'Not guilty!' "

Yes! Elizabeth exclaimed to herself.

The courtroom was buzzing with excitement. But before she knew what was happening, Elizabeth felt arms circling around her. *Ms. Simmons,* she thought hazily, *and Mom and Dad and—*

"An interview, please, with the *Sweet Valley Star*," a gum-chewing reporter said in her ear.

Another flashbulb popped. "How'd you say you spelled your name?" a nasal voice demanded.

"Hey, kid. Not bad!" Steven exclaimed, enveloping Elizabeth in a bear hug as Mandy rushed up to her.

But Elizabeth really wanted to see just one person. Ducking away from the crowd that surrounded her, she headed straight for Joe.

"Elizabeth." Prosthesis still in view, Joe stumbled toward her. With shock, Elizabeth realized there were tears in his eyes. "Thank you, thank you," he muttered, reaching out toward her. "I can't imagine how you could have known—"

"Some other time," Elizabeth told him firmly, hugging him tight. "You're free, that's what counts."

"I—I feel terrible." Joe forced a grin through his tears. "You told me you'd get me out of jail, and I— I just didn't believe you." He shook his head sadly.

Elizabeth stifled a grin as the cameras clicked away in the background. "You know what?"

"What?" Joe asked.

"I didn't always believe me, either," she admitted, giving him another hug.

Thirteen

◇

"Delicious," Maria said, taking a long sip from her soda.

"Mmm hmm," Jessica responded happily, her mouth full of vanilla nut fudge ice cream. It was a Saturday afternoon about two weeks after the trial, and she and Elizabeth and a bunch of their friends were sitting at Casey's counter once again.

"There must be fourteen scoops of ice cream in here," Maria continued. "Joe, I can't imagine what we'd do without you."

"If it weren't for Elizabeth," Amy broke in, "we'd have found out!" She grinned at Elizabeth. "By the way, have I told you how totally amazing it is that you put it all together?"

Elizabeth giggled. "Well, not in a couple of hours . . ."

Maria leaned forward. "Give us the details one more time."

Elizabeth smiled shyly. "Well—"

"Do we have to hear the story again?" Jessica interrupted, shaking her head. "What would this be, the fifty gazillionth time or something?"

"Oh, Jess," Elizabeth said, grinning at her sister. "Aren't you glad to have Joe back here again?"

Jessica stabbed her straw into her milk shake. It stood up tall and straight. "Of course I am," she grumbled. "It's just that I get tired of hearing about how great you are, all right?" It seemed to Jessica as if no one wanted to talk about anything except Elizabeth and her heroics anymore.

Elizabeth laughed. "Actually, I got the idea from something that you said, Jessica."

Jessica pricked up her ears. This was something new. "Oh yeah? What was that?" She had no idea what she'd said, but she was beginning to feel a little proud. *It's about time you recognized the part I played, Lizzie,* she thought, sitting up a little straighter.

"Don't you remember?" Elizabeth turned to her sister. "The puzzle? You know, the brainteaser you told me?"

The brainteaser? Jessica narrowed her eyes and stared. "Huh?" she said.

"The brainteaser," Elizabeth repeated. "You know. The one about the woman who had her tooth pulled?"

Jessica's eyes lit up. "Oh, *that* one," she said importantly. "That's right," she agreed, looking quickly around the group. "That puzzle was the real turning point of the case. I kind of suspected it all along." She tossed her hair behind her shoulders. "You know, that Joe might have had an artificial leg. So I sort of gave Elizabeth a hint."

"Sure thing, Jessica," Lila murmured in a bored voice, then turned back to Elizabeth.

Jessica tried to come up with a good response, but Elizabeth began speaking again.

"Jessica told me a puzzle about a woman who'd lost a part of her body," Elizabeth explained. "Suddenly the pieces all fit together. I realized that if Joe had lost a leg, a lot of things might make more sense."

"And you were right." Joe leaned over the counter and grinned at Elizabeth. "I had no idea you'd done so much research. Going through the old newspapers and talking to people who knew me—" He shook his head and gave a low whistle. "If I'm ever in trouble again, you can guess what detective I'm going to call."

"Oh, stop it," Elizabeth protested, but Jessica noticed that her twin was blushing.

"There's one thing I still don't understand." Mandy twisted back and forth in her stool, licking her ice cream cone. "I know they finally found Jeff's fingerprints on the gun and everything, and I hear he's going to be found guilty for the robbery—"

"He will be," Lila interrupted. "My dad has a friend who knows this guy in the sheriff's department, and—"

"But I still don't understand why," Mandy went on, ignoring Lila. "I mean, he didn't need the money, did he?"

"He did it out of greed." A voice boomed through the store. Jessica sat up quickly and looked for its owner. *Old Mr. Casey,* she thought with surprise. *Only he doesn't look quite so old anymore.*

Mr. Casey came up to the counter and put his arm around Joe's shoulder. "Quite a terrible story," he told them with a sigh. "Turns out that my nephew was desperate to inherit this store when I retired." He shook his head. "I guess I misjudged Jeff—badly. The boy saw how much I liked Joe, here, and he decided he'd better do something about it."

Elizabeth's eyes flashed. "So he took Joe's spare key that was hanging here in the broom closet." She turned toward Joe. "Then he sneaked into your apartment and took your clown suit. Later on, he committed the robbery, hoping you'd be arrested. I should have known," she added, sipping thoughtfully on her root beer float. "You always put your face paint on perfectly. But the clown who robbed the pharmacy? His makeup was on a little crooked. I guess Jeff just didn't know how."

Jessica rested her chin on her fist. How could she have ignored something like that? Now that she thought about it, what Elizabeth said made sense. "That's right," she said aloud. "It *was* on a little crooked."

"Well, I'm delighted Jeff's plot didn't work out," Mr. Casey said happily, clapping Joe on the back. "And I've got an announcement to make. I'm going to be retiring early next year—after a certain person is done with his studies at college."

"Mr. Casey!" Amy wailed.

"Yes," Mr. Casey went on. "But you don't need to worry. I'm going to leave my ice cream parlor in the hands of the most capable person I know." With a quick motion he seized Joe's arm and held it in the air like a champion boxer.

"Mr. Joe Carrey!"

"So I guess we can get back to normal again now," Jessica said hopefully, "since this whole detective case is over." She and Elizabeth were walking home from Casey's later that afternoon.

"Oh, well," Elizabeth mumbled, giving her twin a slight smile. "You never know. I liked being a detective. Maybe more cases will come along."

"Maybe." Jessica shrugged. "But this one's done with, anyway." *And I don't think I ever want to hear about it again.*

"Not quite." Elizabeth's eyes twinkled. "I guess I didn't have a chance to tell you yet about the phone call I got this morning?"

"What phone call?" Jessica turned to face her sister.

"It was from the company that makes those maxipads," Elizabeth replied. "You know, the ones we were trying to buy that night?"

Jessica knew, all right. "And?" she asked impatiently.

"So they heard about the case," Elizabeth went on, "and all about how they had kind of helped to solve it. And they'd talked to the police department and gotten a copy of the tape of the holdup."

Jessica winced. Even now, she didn't like thinking about that videotape. "So what?"

Elizabeth grinned. "So they want me to be a spokeswoman for their product," she said happily. "Isn't that neat? On television commercials!"

Commercials? "Local TV commercials, of course?" Jessica asked, thinking of the stations that were carried on only two or three cable systems around the area.

"Well—not exactly." Elizabeth gave a little shrug. "Network TV, actually. You know, nationwide."

"National TV?" Jessica stared at her sister in astonishment. "They're going to put you on national TV?"

"Uh-huh." Elizabeth nodded. "They're going to give me a lot of money to put away for college," she went on. "They're thinking of doing some kind of advertising slogan like 'You never know when our product might come in handy!' Isn't that funny?"

Jessica frowned. She wanted to be happy for her

sister, but something wouldn't let her. Something that felt a lot like envy. "So, umm, do you think they'll be giving you a glamorous makeover?" she asked cautiously.

"Probably," Elizabeth agreed modestly.

Jessica narrowed her eyes. She couldn't stand it anymore. "You know, Lizzie, I would appreciate that kind of thing a lot more than you would. I mean, you don't care about makeovers! It's not your dream to be on national TV!"

Elizabeth smiled. "I know," she admitted. "But I think it'll be a lot of fun, anyway. I'll be going to a real live studio and everything."

That did it. Jessica zoomed forward, and Elizabeth had to run to keep up with her.

"I can't believe it!" Jessica said loudly, even though Elizabeth was right next to her. "All my life I've been wanting to meet great movie stars, and you'll probably get to meet them, and you won't even know how lucky you are! You'll probably just say, 'Oh, nice to meet you' or something totally dorky like that!" Jessica clenched her fists at the unfairness of it all. "*I'm* the one in the family who deserves to get a studio makeover and meet all the movie stars!"

Elizabeth looked pleadingly at her sister. "But Jess—"

"And besides, I was the one on the video!" Jessica broke in furiously. "It should be *me* getting all that money! It should be *me* in those commercials! It should—"

"Jessica." Elizabeth laid her arm on her sister's shoulder, bringing her to a halt. "Don't make me remind you why it *isn't* you who got the offer for those commercials."

Jessica opened her mouth to speak. But then she closed it again. All of a sudden, her face felt strangely hot.

Elizabeth was staring seriously into her eyes. "After all, Jess—"

"OK," Jessica broke in quickly. She didn't like where this conversation was heading. "I see your point." She cleared her throat. "Congratulations, Lizzie. Only—could you do me one little favor?"

Elizabeth folded her arms. "What's that?"

Jessica smiled sweetly. "Could you get a few autographs for me?"

"Are you ready for another mystery, Detective Wakefield?" Amy asked Elizabeth on Sunday evening.

Elizabeth laughed. The girls were going on a short bike ride before dinner. "Actually, I think I'm going to take a break from detective work for the time being." She glanced at Amy. "Unless you know about a really, *really* good mystery."

Amy wiggled her eyebrows. "*Well*, since you asked, there *is* something kind of strange going on. You know that old Sullivan mansion up on the hill?"

Elizabeth shivered. "How could I not know? That place gives me the creeps. It's been empty for ages."

"That's just it." Amy's voice was low as the girls stopped at a stop sign. "Last night my parents were in that neighborhood for a party, and they said there were lights shining from the windows. Someone must have moved in."

Elizabeth's eyes widened. "Who on earth would want to live in that scary old place?"

Created by FRANCINE PASCAL

Ask your bookseller for any titles you have missed. The Sweet Valley Twins series is published by Bantam Books.

SWEET VALLEY TWINS™

We hope you enjoyed reading this book. If you would like to receive further information about available titles in the Bantam series, just write to the address below, with your name and address:

KIM PRIOR
Bantam Books
61–63 Uxbridge Road
London W5 5SA

If you live in Australia or New Zealand and would like more information about the series, please write to:

SALLY PORTER
Transworld Publishers (Australia) Pty Ltd
15–25 Helles Avenue
Moorebank
NSW 2170
AUSTRALIA

KIRI MARTIN
Transworld Publishers (NZ) Ltd
3 William Pickering Drive
Albany
Auckland
NEW ZEALAND

All Transworld titles are available by post from:-
Bookservice by Post
PO Box 29
Douglas
Isle of Man
IM99 1BQ

Credit Cards accepted.
Please telephone 01624 675137 or fax 01624 670923
or Internet http://www.bookpost.co.uk
or e-mail: bookshop@enterprise.net for details.

Free postage and packing in the UK.
Overseas customers allow £1 per book (paperbacks)
and £3 per book (hardbacks)